# Disaster Bunnies Save THE Day!
## (Kind of)

Look out for the hilarious

# Aliens don't Eat Dog food

# Disaster Bunnies Save the Day! (Kind of)

## Dinah Capparucci

SCHOLASTIC

**JF**

First published in the UK in 2009 by Scholastic Children's Books
An imprint of Scholastic Ltd
Euston House, 24 Eversholt Street
London, NW1 1DB, UK
Registered office: Westfield Road, Southam, Warwickshire, CV47 0RA
SCHOLASTIC and associated logos are trademarks and or registered
trademarks of Scholastic Inc.

ISBN 978 1 407 10810 0

A CIP catalogue record for this book is
available from the British Library

Printed by CPI Bookmarque, Croydon, CR0 4TD
Papers used by Scholastic Children's Books are made from
wood grown in sustainable forests.

1 3 5 7 9 10 8 6 4 2

www.scholastic.co.uk/zone

*With love to all the lonely kids*

*Special thanks to Dan Scriven,
Jack and Luke Sambrook for all their help
researching computer games.*

My name is Jordan and my mate's name is Boy Dave (because his dad is Big Dave). To begin with I should say that none of this was our fault, except maybe what happened to Davina's princess bedroom, which was really an act of mercy anyway, in so much as we put it out of its misery. The rest of what happened was complicated and there were quite a few small and different groups involved, including some Girl Guides, the Easter Parade judges, a stick-wielding maniac and a depressed Polish bloke (who was almost beheaded by the stick-wielding maniac). It would probably take a bit long to list them all but, as usual, many gave in to hysteria and completely overreacted.

Our dads seemed to think we should have learned from our past mistakes, but learning from your mistakes only works if they were quite small and didn't matter much in the first place. Big mistakes are nearly always one-off quite public events and even if you wanted to make them again it would be really difficult to arrange because people would try and stop you. All we learned this time around is that Girl Guides are terrible and a lot of yoga people are not at all chilled out like they're meant to be. We did find out that some people aren't always what you think they are, but that wasn't much use. Most of the time we're in enough trouble as it is without going round being really trusting of bad people and totally paranoid about everyone else.

Anyway – coming back to the beginning – everything really began with the new kid, TC, who started at our school in February.

As everyone knows, February is a pointless month. It's cold and boring; all the excitingness of Christmas has fizzled out. The only event is Valentine's Day, which, so far as I can see, mostly causes big rows and is a bit embarrassing for anyone who tries to take part. Point being, by the last week of February we were desperate for something to happen, and TC's welcome party (as they were calling it) seemed extra exciting because of this.

Where we live is a small, gossipy place and everyone knew about TC way before he knew about them. His family had moved into one of four large houses on the edge of our village. They have big gardens that are closed off by high walls, and long crunchy driveways up to the doors. A few years ago me, Boy Dave and our other mate, Ryan, used to climb over and play in the bushes, but we hadn't been up there for ages.

The Cedars, which is the house TC moved into, used to be owned by three old ladies who always wore black coats and hats and died one at a time, but quite close together so you always had to look to see how many there were. When there had been no sightings of the last one for a while, it was time to fear the worst. We used to call them the Lavatories after the song ("Oh dear, what can the matter be, three old ladies locked in the lavatory", etc.), but after the first one disappeared we felt it was a bit inappropriate until they'd all died and then we started calling them it again. TC's party at the Lavatories' old house was the first time we'd seen inside for years.

As we walked up the hill to the party there were lots of little dots of people ahead of us. I remember thinking it was a bit creepy – like the start of a film where American kids get invited to a big house and are really happy and excited until the bad things start happening.

It was extra weird for us because me and Boy Dave don't normally get invited to parties. Generally speaking, things quite often go wrong and the parents don't like it. Also when you get to our age, which is twelve, it's normally outings like ten-pin bowling or paintballing, and the mums and dads go, "You have to choose only five of your best friends." And then they go, "No, not them. Not him. Definitely not him", until you realize that what they really meant was five people in deep comas who won't be a problem in the car on the way home. Anyway, me and Boy Dave aren't allowed on party outings any more and this was something to do with a big blue inflatable slide, which is a bit long to explain.

When we got to TC's gate, a man in a gorilla suit said, "Invitations?" in a bored voice and gave us each a *TC's Party* balloon.

The funny thing was, we really had been given invitations this time. TC had puffed podgily up to us at school and said in his blocked-nose voice, as if he'd said it a hundred times before, "You're invited to my welcome party." Then he'd given us all a card.

Unfortunately, by the time it got to the day of the party me and Boy Dave (on a scale of one to ten of being grounded) were on ten-plus of total incarceration, with a bit of solitary confinement thrown in. As we had tried to explain (in between all the ranting and yelling), our dads wouldn't have got 10p in a car boot sale for their ancient old record players, and if they'd bought us proper decks, none of this would have happened. But, as usual, there was no reasoning with them.

Still, for once it seemed that luck was on our side.

Just after lunch that Saturday, my mum, dad and sister, Joanna (who is fifteen), had all got dressed up and gone out. Ten minutes later Boy Dave rang to say his had gone as well. That only left my Great Auntie Dulcie, who was sitting at the table in the living room doing what she calls "catching up on her correspondence".

I tiptoed past the living room door and grabbed my trainers and was almost out of the door when she said, "I'm supposed to be keeping an eye on you, Jordan, dear."

My trainers dropped to the floor with a dismal clunk.

"On the other hand," she said in a thoughtful voice, "I am very old and slightly deaf and it's probably rather a lot to expect of someone my age."

"Can I get you anything before I go?" I asked politely.

Dulcie eyed the bottle of brown yuck which she calls *my-dear-ah*. "No thank you, dear, I'm all stocked up."

Minutes later, like a prisoner scenting freedom for the first time in years, I staggered blinking into the daylight.

"I expect they've all gone off on one of their boring trips to the seaside," said Boy Dave when I met him and Ryan at Hangman's Lane. "As long we're back before them, we'll be OK."

Mine and Boy Dave's dads are best mates and our families quite often go on trips to the seaside together – although maybe not so much in February.

"It's quite a long time since we've been invited to a party as well," said Ryan. He pushed his glasses up his nose. "If this one goes well, we might even get invited to some more."

It wasn't until the gorilla at the gate actually asked for the invitations that we realized we'd lost them. We started on all the usual "dog was sick on it" stuff, but he just looked even more bored and waved us through anyway.

Almost straightaway the creepy feeling I'd had earlier turned to excitement. It was obviously a really big do. The path was lined on either side with strings of coloured lights, and from somewhere behind the house was coming the *thump, thump* of music. Giant polystyrene monster footprints with *TC's Welcome Party* written on them led down the side path to the back garden.

It was like walking into a hot kitchen. The courtyard was full of those tall gas heaters that look like lamp posts, and the air smelled of the burgers sizzling on the giant barbecue. Over on the lawn an enormous white tent was thumping out the music we'd heard as we arrived.

"He's invited a lot of little girls to his party," I said, trying not to fall over the hundreds of small,

6

screeching fairy-like people who kept darting out in front of us.

"Huh!" said Boy Dave. "I knew he wasn't our sort of person from the off."

"It's not just fairies he's invited," said Ryan, and there was a bit of edge to his voice. "Take a look around."

Beneath the gazebo, Isaac, the disease-ridden old man from the only (always closed due to illness) village shop was chatting to Andy, the grumpy landlord from the Black Horse pub (who never stops going on about what happened to his satellite dish and who has dedicated his whole life to stopping us having a go on the rowing boats on the stream behind his pub). Just emerging from the tent, some members of the village hall committee (evil sect) were swapping malicious gossip with a cackle of old hags from the Women's Institute (which is really a thinly disguised coven of witches – if ever you are struck down with a nasty rash or cows start producing sour milk, it's most likely down to them). Even the vicious vicar was there by the chocolate fountain, devising righteous punishments with PC White, the local policeman.

Not content with inviting every kid in the school, TC seemed to have invited the whole village! Me and Boy Dave swivelled our eyes from one group to the other with a sense of impending doom.

"Oh boy," said Boy Dave in a low voice, "there are some seriously bad combinations of our enemies here."

"I don't want to alarm you . . ." Ryan was peering over towards the seating area by the barbeque, "but it looks like they aren't the only ones who were invited."

It was the worst possible thing that can happen to any kid at a party. Especially one who's meant to be grounded. Sitting at a plastic table were mine and Boy Dave's mums.

Actually it was the second worst. The first worst was what we noticed straight after that.

Happily chomping away on hot dogs at the same table were our form teacher, Miss Fairjoy, and (super worst) a dumpy figure in an old-fashioned green check skirt and jacket: the headmistress from our school, Miss Stormberry.

"What are *they* doing here?" I whispered hoarsely, when I regained the power of speech.

The fairies – well, they had been in poor taste and a little weird, but harmless enough if you didn't fall over them. The grown-ups – OK, a bad mistake that showed exceptionally poor judgement, but TC was new in town. Perhaps he'd once made friends with a grown-up, and it had warped his thinking a little. But teachers *and* parents. Together. At the same party. . .

Even a raving lunatic couldn't have thought that one up!

"We'll have to create a diversion," said Boy Dave, "before they have a chance to swap accusations and lies."

"I don't think a diversion would work," said Ryan grimly. "This is a pretty hostile environment. It might be best not to draw attention to ourselves."

"Yeah, *your* mum might even be here." I had the feeling that, as usual, Ryan was getting off a bit lightly.

"I don't think so. She's in the middle of one of her metal sculptures. When I left she was welding a lamp post to a car bonnet. It's called 'Giraffe'."

Me and Boy Dave sighed enviously. Ryan's mum is artistic (to put it kindly) and seriously batty. From Ryan's point of view this is great. Even when we're in the sort of trouble that gets me and Boy Dave grounded for weeks, she forgets all about it the next day, so Ryan gets off scot-free. Also he really likes schoolwork, especially science, so his parent/teacher conversations tend to be a lot different to ours anyway.

"Well," I decided to try and be positive, "now we're here we may as well get something to eat and just keep out of everyone's way."

"Yeah," said Boy Dave grumpily. "Right. Great party this is turning out to be."

Luckily, at that moment Connor Keefe and Cal Mockford from our class at school came out of the big white tent. They had the hugest plates of food we'd ever seen. Even Boy Dave goggled at the sight of all their mouth-watering goodies.

"Luckily" isn't a word you would normally think of when you see Connor, and we mostly avoid him. Not so much because he's a bully (although he is), but just because talking to him is like trying to eat custard with a fork.

"All right?" we said with unusual politeness.

"Ulum." Connor's mouth was so crammed full that it was a miracle he hadn't suffocated.

"Is that where we get the food?" I asked, nodding towards the tent.

"Yes, but you have to go through the girls first," said Cal, clearly enjoying being the bringer of bad news. "They're dancing in the middle of the floor."

We looked at each other nervously. If you even so much as glance at girls when they're dancing, they say, "Come . . . come and join the dance." And crowd round you like terrible insects that spit paralysing slime and bind you in webbing and trample on you until all that's left is gunk. On the other hand, there were these great-looking mountains of food to be had. Our tummies rumbled.

"I suppose," I said, without much hope, "there's no other way of getting to the food?"

"Nope." Cal looked smug. "It's like a swarm of piranhas in there."

We decided the best thing would be to sneak in under the edge of the tent at the back. With a quick look round we walked casually up the side, but then Ryan, who was first round the corner, backed up speedily.

"Uh oh, it's Baggers and White."

Me and Boy Dave groaned. It seemed like there wasn't even the tiniest corner of this party that was safe. Mrs Bagnal and Mrs White (who is PC White's mum, by the way) are our two worst enemies of the Women's Institute. They had obviously hidden round there to gobble down all the cakes they had managed to snaffle. We were facing a bad choice: girls dancing or a pair of cake-umphing witches. No-brainer, really. We slid round the corner of the tent and Baggers gave us a shrivel-to-toad stare.

"Where do you think you're going?"

"You're not meant to be here." Mrs White spattered us with damp crumbs. "Go away."

"We're chasing a huge mouse," I told her nicely, "with a really long tail and fangs and. . ."

Strangely for such hardened practisers of the dark arts, Baggers and White looked round nervously.

"And there he goes!" yelled Boy Dave as we dived through their fat and veiny legs under the side of the tent.

We came in right behind the food table as planned, but one of the WI cacklers had managed to grab my ankle and I was still wriggling round on the floor trying to kick her when a hearty-sounding voice said, "Couldn't wait to get at the nosh, eh? Had to dig your way in, ha, ha."

Towering over us was a grown-up, healthier-looking version of TC. His accent wasn't American, exactly; more like someone trying to sound American. The real TC had his back to us and was eating peanuts from a big bowl.

"TC." The big American-ish version tapped the top of the smaller TC's head. "Introduce me to your guests."

TC turned round slowly and gave us the kind of look that you give to certain sorts of maths questions that have letters and numbers.

"This is . . . em. . ."

He stopped as if he couldn't be bothered any more, and absent-mindedly ate some more peanuts. The big TC held out his hand.

"Good to meet you. So glad you could make it. I'm Tom, TC's dad."

There was a bit of a gap while we all waited for someone else to do the hand-shaking. Finally Ryan took the plunge.

"Marconi, sir!" He and Tom shook hands massively.

"Fabulous. Fabulous. Lovely place you have here." Ryan nodded at us. "And this is Degarriat and Smithozillo."

TC's mouth dropped open to reveal a load of half-crushed peanuts and we goggled, but Tom (who didn't seem to find anything at all unnatural about any of this) beamed and tried to yank my hand out of its wrist socket.

"Smithozillo! And Degarriat." He winked at Boy Dave. "You go right on ahead and enjoy! Grab some food. Burgers on the barbecue outside!"

There was tons of it: pizza, sausages, all different little pastry things, crisps, chicken drumsticks, French bread chunks and little creamy cakes. As soon as one plate looked like it was getting low, a chef in a white suit and hat came and topped it up with more.

"Degarriat!" Boy Dave hissed disgustedly to Ryan when we were out of earshot. "What was all that about?"

Ryan shrugged.

"It's the whole shaking hands and not hiding from the kids thing – and the whole weird 'welcome party' concept. It's all very American. I thought it would be good if we sounded like we were in a team – like maybe a baseball team with cheerleaders who do little rhymes about our names. After all," he added, "it's the first party we've been invited to since we made the river of blood and damnation with Steven

Longacre's mum's water feature. We want to make a good impression, remember?"

"That's true," I agreed, secretly quite liking the idea of cheerleaders doing little rhymes about us.

"Huh," said Boy Dave to Ryan. "Well, I like the way you got to keep your own name and we had to be Degarriat and Smithozillo."

"Garret and Smith aren't very American-sounding, though," I pointed out, "especially not if we're in the team."

But there wasn't time to argue. Like sharks scenting their prey, slowly and sinisterly, some of the girls from our class had already started to turn. Quickly we slid back out under the tent and searched for somewhere to devour our spoils.

We ended up at the bottom of the garden on some stone steps under an arch. We used to sit there in the Lavatories days in the summertime, when the arch had droopy purple flowers. That day, though, it was twiggy and bare.

As I munched thoughtfully on crisps and pizza, I got to thinking how weird TC's party was turning out to be. Even though it was a really expensive event, with lots of different things going on, there was a depressing atmosphere – as if the whole thing was damp and wet and kind of dragged down somehow.

"Loads to eat," I said at last.

"They must have some money," said Boy Dave knowingly. "That's the sort of barbecue that actually cooks things."

Ryan said thoughtfully, "I wonder if the house has changed much."

We'd only ever been inside The Cedars once. Back then it had been dim, with dusty sunlighty bits and really old furniture with worn-out patterned rugs. The only reason we'd gone inside in the first place was to try and get back some guinea pigs that we'd borrowed for a mini-circus. On that day, the Lavatories had tried to kill us with a broom and then had the cheek to call PC White.

Needless to say, our mums and dads completely overreacted and the guinea pigs managed to lie low for weeks. By the way, for anyone who's interested in unusual animal facts: even though guinea pigs are small and mostly quite fat, they can run like the wind.

"We'll go and have a look round after this," said Boy Dave, who was in a better mood.

As we made our way back towards the house, I realized what had been bugging me.

"Do you think. . .?" I stopped and tried again. "That Tom – TC's dad – it's like it's really his party and not TC's?"

We looked up the garden to where a lot of grown-ups (grown-ups and fairies) and a few of our class

17

were standing round eating their food awkwardly. The others nodded seriously, and I think for a minute we all felt a bit sorry for TC. Which probably sounds strange if you weren't actually there – what with his massive party, big house and all.

The garden door to The Cedars was open, but there was no one around. When the Lavatories had lived there, the kitchen had been a long, thin room right at the back of the house, with cobwebby shelves, little curtains instead of cupboard doors, and an old square sink. That room was empty now except for a washing machine and spin dryer. The actual kitchen had been moved to the big room behind.

My mum's always moaning about our kitchen. She won't let anyone in when she's cooking because it's so small, but it's quite cosy in there and always smells of whatever's for dinner. TC's kitchen was black and silver and about five times the size of ours. As you went in there was a long glass dining table straight ahead, with the main kitchen to the right, like a thick T-shape. It was this main kitchen bit that got our attention. There, in the middle, like a sort of magnificent sculpture on a silver trolley, was the most amazing food we had ever seen.

"Profiteroles," whispered Ryan after a moment of silent worshipping.

Piled high, from our waists to our heads, were hundreds of little doughy balls oozing with cream. A waterfall (or really a chocolatefall) of chocolate sauce had set into thin glistening streams, which had trickled down the sides, making a thick, shiny puddle at the bottom. We inched closer and the air became saturated with the hypnotizing smell of cake shops and melted chocolate.

It was a once-in-a-lifetime opportunity.

"We'll only have a few," said Boy Dave dreamily, "and then rearrange it the same as it was."

"It seems to me," said Ryan, his glasses dazzling in the chocolate shine, "that if we take from the top we'll have to make it back into a mountain shape, which will be messy. On the other hand, if we just took the whole bottom layer, it would just be like moving it down a notch."

"Or two," we agreed.

The bottom layers were quite squashed already, so as soon as we took one out it was easy to just squish down the one above a bit. Obviously, everything went a bit wonky to begin with, but we reckoned once we'd eaten all the way round it would be fine. At least that was the plan.

It was all going quite well. We'd had about five profiteroles each and were about to go into the second half to even things out when a noise made us jump. It was the click of the back door opening.

We looked around. In a film there would have been a handy cupboard where we could have hidden and witnessed something that would change our lives for ever. In reality, and based on a previous disastrous hiding effort (you see, bad mistakes don't happen twice), kitchen cupboards are always really full up – and even if these weren't, there was no way we'd all have time to cram in.

Desperately trying to swallow our huge mouthfuls of chocolate and cream, we scuttled back towards the table. By now voices were drifting through what used to be the old kitchen and heading our way. There was no getting back through that door. Our only chance was to scramble through the one leading into the rest of the house.

We made it just as the voices entered.

"Ever since we moved here," a nervous-sounding woman's voice was saying, "I've had a . . . sense . . . you know? That there was a poor departed soul trying to contact me from the other side. Sometimes I'll just be standing there and feel a kind of . . . presence. . ."

Cautiously we poked our heads round the door. The one talking was an unnatural orangey-brown colour with perfect-looking hair, like a shop dummy. I supposed this must be TC's mum. The other was fleshy and large, with bright red fish lips and colourful, flowing clothes.

"And when you felt this presence," asked the flowing one in a concerned-sounding voice, "did you notice that the temperature in the room changed in any way? Perhaps you felt colder – as if there was a sudden chill in the air?"

"Oh yes," said the one who must be TC's mum, "*icy* cold. And sometimes, I've even caught a *glimpse*, you know, of a grey, shrouded figure. And it seemed to be . . . reaching out to me, like a poor tormented soul begging for help. That's why I'm so glad you could come. I just know that there is a poor lost spirit residing here that needs our help to move on."

"Yes," nodded the flowing one absent-mindedly. She had noticed the profiterole mountain. "As an experienced medium and spiritual healer, I can tell, just by walking" (licking her lips, she drifted nearer the trolley) "into your home, that there is a most unnatural energy. But my!" She gave up drifting and bustled towards it. "This looks delicious."

TC's mum folded her arms and gazed at the profiterole mountain proudly. "It's our desert *finale*. I'm just going to put some sparklers on it before I present it to the guests. While I'm doing that you could take a look round the house," she suggested eagerly, "and see where all the ghosts are."

"Spirits," said the medium irritably, withdrawing the finger that she had been about to dip. "We call them spirits."

I expect her heart was sinking as fast as ours. A few moments later we heard the fizzing of sparklers, then TC's mum, holding high the profiterole platter, started back for the garden.

The profiteroles went quite gradually at first. As TC's mum made her way gingerly down the steps of the courtyard into the garden, a few stragglers rolled down and bounced off, splatting on the ground. Still, this didn't make too much difference, and the guests all stopped what they were doing and went "Ooooh" and "Ahhh", and some started to applaud.

Maybe it was the vibrations of the clapping, but more and more of the profiteroles bounced off. Panicking, TC's mum started to do little running steps, but the running must have made it worse because the mountain seemed to reach a sort of critical point of lopsidedness and there was a sudden profiterole landslide.

It was like a cartoon person where the person's legs stretch and go all bendy. TC's mum twisted and swerved as she tried to do a sort of ball-in-the-cone catch with the tray, but she must've slipped on one because the next thing we knew, she was sitting on the ground and the rest of it had collapsed on her head.

"Ohhhhhhhh," went the partygoers disappointedly, while TC's mum, hair sizzling with sparklers, let out a muffled shriek, "such a shame."

Some quick-thinking ones rushed over and dabbed feebly with serviettes, and the medium also rushed over and ate a few off her face. Meanwhile, we slid back into the shadows.

"It wasn't our fault," I told the others as we had a look round the rest of the house.

Ryan nodded. "And if they hadn't interrupted us, we could have eaten it a bit more evenly."

We were on our way upstairs. The large rooms downstairs had been full of perfect-looking furniture and un-walked-on rugs, almost like a show house where no one actually lived. When the Lavatories lived in The Cedars, it had been decorated with wooden African-type animals and some really *weird* china dogs' heads on the wall, but at least it was like an actual home.

On the main landing, two smaller flights led to left and right corridors, and another narrower staircase curled round behind us.

"That would have been for the servants in the old days," said Ryan. "Their rooms would have been at the top of the house."

We decided to leave those until last and took the right corridor, but it turned out to be nothing but bedrooms. They would take a bit long to describe, except to say that each one had its own bathroom and was a particular colour, like pink or blue.

The opposite corridor was a bit more interesting. There was a purple and gold bedroom, which we decided was TC's mum and dad's because there were some dressing gowns with gold initials on the door. Leading off the bedroom was a bathroom with a floor bath, like a mini swimming pool, and huge taps in the shape of fish.

"I dunno." Boy Dave looked at the loo, which had a matching fish handle. "They must spend their whole time in the bath or on the bog."

"It's quite likely to be some sort of congenital disease," said Ryan in his scientific voice, "which means they must never be far away from the nearest toilet."

While they tried to decide what different diseases TC's family might have, I noticed another door on the other side of the bathroom.

"Come and have a look at this!" I called to the others. "I think I've finally found something interesting."

Looking back on it – although as it turned out, there were a few moments you could say this about – I still think this was where our problems really began.

Boy Dave and Ryan crowded in over my shoulders.

"Wow!" said Boy Dave. "Sauna and jacuzzi!"

There was a rail of white towels, and gleaming tiles on all the walls and floor. Along one side was a sort of wooden hut and, a little bit away, a massive round tub. Cautiously we crept over, and Ryan pushed the button on the side of the jacuzzi. The water started to gurgle and bubble like a monster blowing through a straw.

"I've always wanted to have a go of one of these," said Ryan excitedly.

"We'd best not," I said. Me and Boy Dave had actually had a go of one on holiday, but a woman complained that she couldn't relax because we were pretending it was our farts making all the bubbles. "Knowing our luck, someone's bound to come in, and then we'd have to run away with no clothes on."

"True," agreed Boy Dave, "and then we might not get invited to any more parties."

"If we just had a quick go in the sauna, then?"

suggested Ryan. "We could keep our clothes on for that."

We had just opened the little wooden door and peeked into what looked like a cosy, dim shed when we heard a strange noise: *tap tap. Tap, tap tap.* As if someone was tapping gently on the wall of TC's mum and dad's bathroom.

The gentle tapping grew louder: *bang. Bang!*

We looked at each other with round eyes. Perhaps TC's mum had been right. Maybe the house really was haunted. Maybe it was the Lavatories in there banging warningly with a ghost broom.

Slowly we turned round and, at the same time, so did the door handle from the bathroom.

"Chipboard," said a familiar voice. "These wouldn't have been in the original building."

Not ghosts!

Worse than ghosts.

The colour drained from mine and Boy Dave's faces.

"So what've they put in here, then?"

The door opened further, but by this time we were bolting for our lives through the other door into the corridor.

"Well," I heard my dad say (I suppose he'd just seen the jacuzzi), "this is the high life, isn't it?"

We should have realized when we heard the tapping. Our dads own a building company called Rise Building Contractors, and there's nothing they like better than nosing round houses and tapping the walls to see if they're hollow (and no, I really don't know why this should be). They had obviously got bored with the party and decided to look round instead.

"We'd better go back to the party," whispered Boy

Dave as we headed for the stairs, "and carry on lying low. If they find out we've come out, they'll be really mad."

I nodded gloomily. "And it might be best not to be connected with the profiterole thing either."

"No one could blame us for that," said Ryan in a superior way. "That was just the force of gravity."

Me and Boy Dave gave him a look.

"We get blamed for the force of gravity," I told him, "along with everything else."

We were just about to start down the stairs when voices drifted up from the hall below.

"Like, when I'm older I'll have my house like this, only with silver and pale blue in the living room?"

"Or maybe *gold*?"

"Yuh, but if I had gold it would have to be, like, more of a green on the walls? And, like, I'm more of a pale blue person?"

There are only two people in the world who could be having such a mind-curdlingly ridiculous conversation made up completely of questions: my sister, Joanna, and her stupid friend Collette.

We hovered on the landing wondering whether to go down or not. After all, Joanna and Collette shouldn't be nosing round the house either. On the other hand, they hadn't been grounded until the next millennium like we had. And it's a fact that Joanna has a megalodon-sized gob when it comes to grassing people up.

The sound of the sauna door opening made up our minds for us. As we scuttled back down the corridor, I started to feel like this was some sort of terrible experiment set up by TC: invite all our enemies and families to a party and see how long we lasted.

There was a sort of sticking-out doorway with purple and gold velvet curtains over the entrance some way down the corridor. It was pretty much our only chance. Throwing the curtains aside, we piled in and pulled them shut tight behind us. Straightaway there was a tinkling, whooshing noise and a soft voice said, *"Welcome to a magical fairyland, where all your wishes really can come true."*

"Oh no!" whispered Boy Dave. "That's all we need. Fairy ghosts!"

Ryan sniffed in a superior sort of way. "I think you'll find it's a recording. We probably triggered the sensors when we came in. Look."

He stuck his hand back out through the curtains. Meanwhile, the sound of the sauna door opening meant our dads were making their way out into the hall.

"Don't *wave* at them!" I hissed at Ryan, trying to yank his arm in.

*"Welcome to a magical fairyland,"* said the voice, *"where. . ."*

The effect was spoiled somewhat by the sound of boots stomping down the corridor. For a terrible moment we pressed ourselves back and held our breath, but luckily the stomping passed on by.

While we waited to give all our annoying family members time to get clear (and had a few more goes of each being welcomed to fairyland), we realized that we were actually squidged up inside a sort of false entrance to another room. The real door was behind us, and on it, in sparkly pink loopy letters, was written *Welcome to Fairytopia*.

"Why don't we have a look in here?" I whispered, trying the door handle. "Until they've all had time to disperse a bit."

Unlike the jacuzzi, this wasn't something I later lived to regret. I regretted it straightaway.

It was like going into a tasteless sort of Narnia. On the whole of the wall opposite the door was a huge scene of purple-topped mountains and unicorns flying, a rainbow in a misty sky and a distant fairy castle. The right wall was covered with an enormous waterfall, which reminded me of the big faded photograph in the Indian takeaway (except with bat-sized butterflies), and at the far end, behind a four-poster bed, was the inside of a castle with a handsome prince waiting at the top of a staircase. Instead of the walls stopping where they were meant to, the uneven horizons on the wallpaper made the room seem disjointed and out of shape.

As I looked around, I realized that even the most normal objects were covered in (mostly pink and purple) feathers and fur. It was like the whole place was crawling with creatures. Even the fur-rimmed alarm clock looked as if it was about to scuttle off at any minute. Whoever slept in the four-poster bed (which was covered with fluffy heart-shaped cushions and Disney-style toys) had obviously taken precautions. Purple and pink mosquito-type netting was bunched all around in case the feather creatures flew in at night, and the posts were strung with multicoloured plastic flower lights.

"This," said Boy Dave after a bit, in an awestruck voice, "is the most hideous room I've ever been in."

"Isn't it *magnificent*?" Ryan had sat down on a mini-throne, and was tucking a fluffy pink rug round his knees. "Cherish the moment. It is the closest we will ever get to pure anti-beauty."

There was a sudden *nei-ei-ei-ei-gh* as Boy Dave strayed too near a life-sized pony. It pretended to chomp sloppily on a plastic carrot.

"Vile, more like," I said.

"Absolutely," agreed Ryan, "but *inspirationally* vile, don't you think?"

"I expect," I swallowed, trying not to look at anything in particular, "our dads have probably gone now."

"When I have a house," said Ryan, who wasn't showing signs of wanting to leave any time soon, "I'm going to have a room like this."

"Well, I won't be coming round yours, then," said Boy Dave disgustedly. "Come on," he said to me. "Let's get out of here. It's making me nauseous."

And that was when we opened the door of Fairytopia and tried to leave.

At this point, as my Auntie Dulcie would say, our nerves were already frayed. But what happened next ripped them to pieces.

A hundred giant, pink-winged, screeching, squawking rats and crows came out of nowhere and stampeded down the corridor. We threw ourselves back inside Fairytopia and slammed the door, but it was too late.

"SQUEEK, SCREETCH, SQUEAL." The door flew open and the creatures swarmed in. They fell upon the things like vultures.

"*Oh!* You've got Peeky Petal Boo!"

"*Oooh!* It's Pony Princess!"

"SQUEEK! It's Make-up-and-Go Fairy Marigold."

"*Screech!* Brand new Party Girl Dress-My-Hair!"

A sudden blood-curdling howl from the doorway shocked them into silence.

Standing in the doorway, wand in hand, was the queen of fairy trolls. She was the ugliest little girl I had ever seen. Whereas Tom had been like a larger, healthier-looking version of TC, she was like a smaller, squatter version. She had a flat face like TC, but his hair was clipped in a really short number two, whereas hers was completely white and stuck out all around her head like tangled spiders' webs. Her fairy corset bulged and strained over her tummy and her face was squished down like a pile of marshmallows. From between the layers she fixed the other fairies with an evil stare.

"THOSE ARE MY FIIIINGS!"

She poked the first fairy really hard with her wand.

"That's *MY* Peeky Petal Boo and *you* are a poo face so *you* can't play with it." She jabbed another fairy in the eye. "It's *MY* Pony Princess and you have wee breath so *you* can't play with it. It's *MY* Make-up-and-Go Fairy Marigold" (scratch, poke) "and you are a plop nose so you can't play with it. It's *MY* Party Girl Dress-My—"

She froze.

On the throne, Ryan gathered his furry covers around him and blinked at her through his glasses.

The troll fairy looked back at him and breathed in. And the breathing in lasted for a very long time. Then, with a diabolical wail, she flew across the room and fell upon him like a terrible bird of prey.

"MY FRONE!" It was like all the chalk on dry blackboards, polystyrene scratches and dentists' drills in the universe joined into one nerve-incinerating screech. "MY FUFFIES! MY PWINCESS CWO-WOWN!"

Ryan, glasses dangling from one ear, tried desperately to stop the wand poking his eyes out, but more and more of the fairies came. Like ravening beasts they mauled and gouged, scratched and tore, until he disappeared beneath a wobbling of wings.

Don't get me wrong. We would have tried to help. But they had fairy magic and star wands, and we were unarmed and outnumbered. And anyway, we were laughing too much.

Halfway up the small winding servants' staircase, I started to feel a bit guilty.

"Maybe we should go back and try and rescue him?"

"No way." Boy Dave gave me a look. "There's millions of them. Anyway, maybe it'll teach him not to enjoy girl stuff so much."

Even then I thought we should have gone back, except we had just arrived at quite an interesting-looking door. *TC's TERRITORY*, said the notice, *KEEP OUT OR ELSE*, and underneath there were some drawings of people being hideously killed if they went in there.

We'd only really meant to poke our heads round and have a quick look, but what happened next was the one thing we'd never have expected. The last time we had seen him he had been stuffing down peanuts in the tent, but now, hunched over in the darkness, we found TC.

The curtains, which were thick and heavy, were drawn tightly shut, and he was sitting on a low gamer's chair completely surrounded by computers and TVs. The butt of his rifle was poking up on the edge of the largest screen and he was busy shooting enemy soldiers.

"*Arghh. Ooff. Howahh aieeee!*" went the soldiers.

"*Ratatatata tatata tatatatatatat,*" went TC on rapid fire.

There was a *click/clunk* as he changed his magazine and carried on firing.

Boy Dave said in a low voice, "Do you think we should go?"

But there was something so weird about it. We could faintly hear the music playing outside. The tables in the tent were probably still laden with food, and before we left, it had looked as if a small circus was setting up – yet here was TC hiding away in the dark at the top of the house.

After a few minutes, when he still hadn't noticed us, I walked over and tapped him on the shoulder. He jumped, swung suddenly round in his chair and tried to shoot me. I did the most obvious thing you can do when someone's going "*ratatatatat*" at you creepily under their breath, and backed off slowly with my hands up.

"Oh." TC lowered his imaginary weapon. "It's you. Smithozillo."

Boy Dave giggled.

"And Degarriat," I said.

TC gave a small, bored nod. Before then I hadn't really noticed what he looked like apart from that he was tubby. Now I saw that he was a bit unreal-looking himself – like he'd transmogrified into half boy, half virtual character, not that you'd choose to be him in a game. His whole face was squashed and flat-looking, with teeny lines for his eyes and mouth. With his short, clipped hair, it was like looking at a bald, white plasticine head that had been dropped face down on the floor.

For a moment me and Boy Dave stood gazing at all the different screens. Each one was set up ready with a different game.

"What are you doing in here?" asked Boy Dave eventually. "Why aren't you outside enjoying your party?"

TC shrugged. "I was bored."

"But surely you can do this any time."

"I enjoy doing this, though," said TC. "I don't enjoy parties."

"You've got a lot of nice gear." I nodded round approvingly.

"Yeah!" TC suddenly brightened up. "I've got it all: XBox 360 – radio-controlled platinum version – PS2, PS3, Nintendo Wii sensor stuff. Want to have a look at my games?"

He pushed his chair back to reveal shelves and shelves of them beneath the desks.

"Wow!" I said. "*Halo 3!*"

"Your mum let you have all this crime stuff?" asked Boy Dave with new respect in his voice.

TC shrugged. "Kind of."

"*Smackdown Vs Raw*." I pulled out a box. "We used to play this. Have you done Buried Alive?"

"WWE? Course. I've done 'em all." TC leaned back knowledgeably in his chair. "Who's your best combatants?"

We went on to have a conversation (which got a bit dull after a bit) about all the different wrestlers in *Smackdown Vs Raw*. And then all the legends and then the different versions and blah blah.

I started to understand why TC needed so many PlayStations and computers. He had practically everything worth having going back over about four years, right up to the very latest.

Me and Boy Dave had a few games between us and sometimes we got into them for a bit, but most of the time we preferred to be out and about. Seemed like

41

TC was the exact opposite – the outside world for a bit and then back inside.

"You can play anything you like," he told us generously. "I've got more chairs, and we can push the tables round to make room."

At the time I didn't really feel much like it, but TC was so enthusiastic, and maybe it was the idea of him all alone up here, but I actually felt a bit sorry for him. We agreed to just have a quick go and then go back and get some more food from the party.

It was about an hour later and my eyes were getting dry when a sudden thought occurred to me. I took a break from being Master Chief and turned to Boy Dave. "Ryan's been gone for ages."

But Boy Dave was blowing up an ambulance with an RPG and didn't seem particularly interested.

"He's probably still in the hideous bedroom."

"We . . . em . . . had a quick look in the pink room when we were looking for you earlier," I said hastily to TC.

"Oh, Davina's Fairytopia." TC nodded gloomily. "She's my sister. She's having her fairy party today as well." He sighed. "And my dad's turned it into his 'greet the village' day as well. I expect you saw them all."

It was good to know that the fairies and grown-ups

were nothing to do with TC, but I was starting to get a niggling feeling.

"We should probably go and find our mate quite soon."

Too late. A long horror-movie scream echoed up from the floor below. TC looked interested again. "What sort of creature is that?"

Me and Boy Dave looked at each other.

"The human sort," said Boy Dave tiredly.

At the time, in the big "seeing the error of our ways" talk from Tom, which I'll come to in a bit, me and Boy Dave didn't know exactly what had happened. Quite a lot of it came out during Tom's long lecture, but we only got the exact details when Ryan told us them later. Basically, after his horrible ordeal, Ryan had decided to relax in the sauna.

I don't think you're meant to stay in a sauna so long that the redness doesn't go down until the next day but, not knowing when he was going to get another go of one, Ryan was determined to make the most of it. He worked out later, from the temperature of the sauna and the average temperature of the Sahara, that he'd done the same as a three-day walk in the desert in forty-five minutes. It might have been longer but he was suddenly overcome with a terrible thirst.

I should say at this point that the next bit wasn't really as bad as TC's mum made out. Ryan can only see blurs without his glasses and he'd had to take them off in the sauna because the metal bits were burning his ears, so the most he would have seen was a shape on the toilet. As he pointed out later, if anyone should have felt "shamelessly violated", it was him.

I think what annoyed TC's mum was that when she yelled out to say she was in the bathroom, Ryan should have gone, "Oops, sorry" and quickly closed the door. But, at the time, the terrible thirst was so terrible that it was all he could think about.

His logic, which was a bit warped by his desert experience, was that if he could just nip in quickly and have a drink from the tap, he could go out again and pretend he hadn't realized anyone else was there. Unfortunately he forgot it was a floor bath and fell in, so to TC's mum it looked as if he'd just rushed in wearing only his pants and jumped in her bath. Luckily she wasn't in it and, to be fair, he was only in there for a very short space of time, so she could probably have got in afterwards – although Ryan was very sweaty at the time and I suppose some of it probably did go in the water.

I think someone got TC's dad, Tom, from the garden, and me and Boy Dave came downstairs, followed by TC, who was a little bit interested to see what had happened, but not very much because it wasn't a game.

By the time we found them in Tom's study, someone had made Ryan put on a yellow bathrobe, and he was sitting wetly in a chair with Tom standing over him. TC's mum, also in her dressing gown, still with bits of profiterole cream in her hair, was leaning against the window sill, pretending to be in a film where she'd been saved from a psychopath at the last minute.

"OK, Marconi," Tom was saying to Ryan sternly, "let's take this from the top. You come and have a look round the house, right? I would have been happy to get someone to show you round, but, number one, it's polite to ask a guy first. So what do we learn from this? ASK SOMEONE FIRST. Number two, you help yourself to our facilities. I would have been only too happy to arrange it, but, hey, this is my son's welcome party and it would be nice if you could respect that – spend some time mixing with the other guests, you know what I mean? So what do we learn from this? THERE'S A TIME AND A PLACE – respect your host. But now, Marconi, we get to the bit I'm not so happy with!" There was a big pause so Ryan could reflect on the error of his ways. "My wife" – Tom drew himself up tall – "takes some time out to wash a little cake from her hair. Hey, I say she deserves to relax after organizing this event so that it goes like clockwork, and guests such as yourself can enjoy our hospitality and entertainment. And they're very welcome, aren't they, Bosie?"

He looked over at TC's mum, who made an "except when they try to murder me in my bathroom" face and said, "If my guests are happy then I'm happy. You know that, dear—"

"BUT," interrupted TC's dad loudly, "to shamelessly violate my wife's privacy in this way is not how we do things round here." He sighed as if we had given him this huge problem to sort out. "Heck – I dunno what sort of rules you play by in your home, but here we do not go into other people's private space uninvited. You hear me, Marconi? We do not take a bath that is intended for someone else. . ."

TC's mum looked miffed and said, "When they're as naked as the day they were born and. . ."

"When they're as naked as the day they were born," agreed TC's dad. "And sitting on the toil—"

"Doing their private business," interrupted TC's mum.

Ryan, who had started to shuffle his feet, obviously wanted to say something – which, from our point of view, was a bit worrying. What TC's dad probably hadn't realized yet is that there are some normal human emotions (such as guilt and embarrassment) that Ryan has never properly understood. This will be useful for when he is a scientist who does experiments wearing protective clothing behind a heavily guarded, steel-plated door, and who only communicates with the outside world to say things like, "The time has come to try the X41 on humans." But Ryan didn't have an intercom or steel-plated door, and he was only wearing a slightly off-putting yellow dressing gown – and the fact that he was trying to say something anyway (which almost certainly wasn't going to be "I'm really sorry and it won't happen again") made it seem quite important to try and shut him up. I coughed loudly.

"Ahem."

"Ahh, Smithozillo!" Tom seemed to notice us for the first time. "You know anything about this?"

I started to get a nasty feeling that this particular excuse would need to be one of those detailed ones that end up needing lots of dodgy add-ons.

"Well . . . yes . . . and yet . . ." (I decided to do what spies do and stick as close to the truth as possible.) ". . . also . . . probably no."

Tom put his fists on his hips and glowered.

"I mean," I continued, "it wasn't really his fault. It was. . ."

"Us," finished Boy Dave. "We left him on his own and. . ."

"He wandered off."

"Because. . ."

"Of his illness!" I finished lamely.

We quite often use illnesses as an excuse. People are always nervous about saying you're making them up, even when they're pretty sure you are.

48

"Yes." Boy Dave folded his arms and nodded sadly. "Em . . . he. . ."

We were both having the same problem. When it came down to it, there didn't seem to be any illnesses that actually fitted the situation. Then I had a brainwave. What if we pretended that Ryan had the same problem as TC's family? They'd probably be really sympathetic.

"It's a con. . ." I tried to think of the name of it.

". . .gealeal. . ." finished Boy Dave. "A nasty bout of congealeal."

"*Congenital*," corrected Ryan grandly. "Congenital disease, which runs in families and is normally present from birth. It. . ."

"*Means*," I glared at him, "that he must never be more than a very short distance away from a toilet."

There was a bit of a silence. Then TC's mum put her hand on her mouth. "Oh my goodness. TC, why didn't you tell us? We could have made arrangements."

TC blinked and Boy Dave said quickly, "He – I mean, poor old Marconi – doesn't like a lot of people to know. It's normally OK because we're always with him, but we were really enjoying spending time with TC, and I'm afraid we didn't notice that he'd run off."

We gazed at Ryan caringly while he peered back as if we were bugs under a microscope.

"I think it would be best," I tried for the long shot, "if we just took him home now."

Ryan, who recognized escape when he saw it, stood up, ready to make a break for it, but Tom held up a hand.

"*Just* a moment."

Ryan sat back down with a thump.

"OK." Tom started to pace the floor. "*So* let's just put the picture into focus. You're meant to be caring for your buddy, who has some sort of disease that runs in his family, right? But then you get talking to TC here and get distracted and Marconi slips off unsupervised to take care of his . . . needs. Am I right so far?"

By this time it was getting really hard to get the picture of Ryan as an incontinent maniac out of my head. Boy Dave must have felt the same, because he had started to go red in the face and nod too much. Luckily Tom, the great detective, took this to mean that he was on the right track.

"BUT," he said cunningly, "it still doesn't explain why, when he was caught, Marconi was only wearing his underpants."

Ryan said helpfully, "When I'm having one of my episodes I quite often get very confused and find I've taken off all my clothes. I don't know why. . ."

"*Or*. . ." Tom held up a finger. ". . .what he was doing in the *pamper suite*."

In the terrible silence that followed, Boy Dave

whimpered and tears started to trickle down my face. I tried to think of sad things but the laughter was like an alien trying to get out of my body. The situation wasn't helped much by the weird flicker that ran suddenly across Tom's face.

"OH!" he said. Then, bravely, "Oh well. I'm sure it's nothing that can't be fixed."

TC's mum suddenly asked brightly, "Who'd like some lemonade?"

Boy Dave, who'd been holding his breath too long, slid down the door frame on to the floor.

I have been thinking lately that probably the best excuses for these sorts of situations are madness and senility. They're the only ones that can explain a long list of things which all happened close together but that were quite different, except that you were involved in all of them. Unfortunately, one of the only times they won't do is when you're twelve years old or you've just done another excuse about being a responsible carer. Luckily, though, TC's mum and dad seemed to take Boy Dave and me laughing as us just being a bit wacky.

TC's mum gave us a bit of an odd smile and said playfully, "Well, I've never seen anyone so pleased to be offered some of my lemonade before."

"So," said Tom, in an amused sort of way, "*you're* TC's new best buddies."

He strode over and put his arm round TC, then changed his mind and punched him playfully instead. "TC's a real magnet. Always the most popular guy in the class, eh, TC? Any of you play golf?" Tom asked suddenly.

"No," we laughed, "no, we don't."

Tom, who was getting swept up in the lemonade spirit, did a creepy smile and raised his eyebrows invitingly. "Would you like to *learn*?"

"Yes," we said joyfully (and as it turned out later, really stupidly), "why not?"

TC, who obviously knew more about these things than we did, stared blankly into space and looked as if he was missing his darkened room.

The worst thing about living in a small village is that everyone gets involved in everything else. I sometimes wonder who the person is that actually wants all the village things to happen – like a demon who takes on human form and infiltrates the community as a member of the village hall committee (actually, this doesn't necessarily need to be in human form) who goes, "I've got a good idea. Let's do a flower show, *an Easter parade*, a fête, a jumble sale, a fun run, or – you're gonna like this one – what say we do them ALL?"

And not one person in the whole village has the courage to jump to their feet and say, "NO! That's a terrible idea and I'll have no part in it! Do your own dirty work and may the crows peck out your eyes for all your devil's ways."

Instead they go, "Hmm, yes, hmm. I suppose I could help with the bric-a-brac."

Then, its evil work done, the demon slides back down a sulphurous crater and we have to put up with our mums going, "Oh, the blooming cake stall/

jumble collection/geraniums in pots/costume-sewing (whatever). I told them I could only do a few hours this year and now I've ended up having to do all this WORK!" Like it's come as a terrible shock and nothing like this has ever happened before.

And then, just because they have to suffer, they expect you to be the same. Even if you manage to get out of being dragged into the village activities at home, they force you to do it at school – just so they can have the glorious moment of a picture in the local paper saying, *Many thanks to all the children of Hatton Down Community School for all their hard work in helping make the* – (whatever depressingly lame event) – *such a huge success.*

Also, my sister, Joanna, is always in the picture, so Mum has a revolting special Joanna scrapbook and drops big hints about having a few of me "getting more involved".

At school that Monday, they were already making plans for the Easter Carnival. This is normally yet another pathetic village event where two farmers' trailers drive down the main street with a goat, a few flowers and a few tragic kids in embarrassing costumes. The Women's Institute (who have to get in on everything) sell a few herbs and potions along the way and eat the odd child in the bushes. The only thing worth going for is the van with the jumbo hot dogs.

Anyway, the school always does get a bit excited about the Easter Carnival because it organizes most of the parade. This year, though, they were extra excited. Actually, change that to ridiculously overexcited.

The atmosphere was as if a tornado was due to hit in twenty-four hours. The staffroom had almost certainly been converted into an emergency nerve centre with huge computer screens and hotline telephones so a team of experts could battle against time. As for the rest of us, we had to go to the school gym, where the headmistress was waiting to prepare us for the worst.

Miss Stormberry (whose actual name I only found out recently) is a bit like a Second World War sort of person, with suits that look as if they're made out of old horse blankets and really dark brown baggy tights.

"Now gather round, everyone!" she said in a jolly voice as we shuffled in. "I would like you to welcome our very special guests, Bill Leafydew and Bonnie Beer. As you all know, Bill Leafydew" (she held out an arm to a man with a long ponytail who nodded boringly) "and Bonnie Beer" (a frumpy-looking woman with glasses also nodded) "are the famous gardeners who will be on the panel of judges for the carnival this year. Now, Bill Leafydew, if I might ask you to say a few words about this exciting event."

Me and Boy Dave groaned. Whenever people are asked to "say a few words", time stretches ahead like a terrible grey road of boring nothingness with no way of knowing when it will ever end.

Bill Leafydew stepped forward and rubbed his hands together cheerfully. "Thank you. Well, first of all, I should ask if there are any keen gardeners amongst you."

"Oh, for crying out loud," muttered Boy Dave, "this is ridiculous."

Ryan obviously didn't agree. His hand shot up.

"Good." Bill Leafydew smiled at him. "That's what we like to see. What sort of things are you growing at the moment, may I ask?"

Ryan peered at him. "I'm quite a long way from that stage. However," he put on his scientific voice, "for some time I've been interested in modifying a number of plant species by using recent advances in science technology which. . ."

Bill Leafydew, who had probably been thinking of normal plants, laughed nervously.

"Ahh! Well!" he said. "I'm not sure we've got enough time to. . ."

"It seems to me," continued Ryan, making his way to the front, "that with careful use of nanotechnology, certain sorts of weed could be modified to completely take over whole continents and release a gas. . ."

"Well, it's, em. . ." Bill Leafydew looked anxiously

back at Bonnie Beer, who shrugged. ". . .an interesting idea, but. . ."

"PLANT WARFARE," interrupted Ryan, "is a most underdeveloped. . ."

The headmistress sighed and shoved Bill Leafydew out of the way.

"Mr *Marconi*!" She fixed Ryan with a stern glare. "I'm sure that the members of the *Gardeners' Answers* panel will be only too happy to discuss this with you after we have finished. For the time being, Mr Leafydew is going to explain to you all about the far more important matter of the Easter Carnival parade!"

Bill Leafydew wiped his forehead.

"Good," he said. "Right! Now, as I'm sure you all know, the famous radio programme *Gardeners' Answers* hosts a very prestigious garden party every year. Myself and Bonnie" (he waved an arm towards Bonnie Beer, who nodded again, but this time a bit more enthusiastically) "are going around the country judging various village events. We will be using these opportunities to decide which village or town should be chosen to host our very prestigious garden party next year. Most importantly, next year's garden party is to be especially prestigious because the QUEEN has very graciously accepted an invitation!"

He paused, waiting for this amazing news to sink in. Which was strange, considering we were sixty years too young to get excited about royalty. Mistaking the coma-like silence for awe, he carried on. "As well as the prestige such an event would bring to the village, it will provide a wonderful opportunity for. . ."

By now the headmistress had obviously decided that far too much had been said about prestige already and it was about time he got down to the nitty-gritty.

"There's a good chance the village will make a great deal of money out of it," she said, elbowing Bill Leafydew out of the way. "The Women's Institute will be able to sell refreshments; the bed and breakfasts will be jam-packed. The school will do display thingies and concerts and have its own taxi rank, and I daresay some of our more enterprising pupils may have a few ideas of their own to add. Therefore, it is imperative we do our very best to make sure that this year's Easter Carnival is a spectacular success." She looked round meaningfully. "And we here at Hatton Down Community School must ensure that *our* contribution to the Easter Parade is a shining tribute to the school!" She began a pathetic round of applause for Bill Leafydew and Bonnie Beer before telling them the good news. "Mr Marconi will show you round the school. Ryan is one of our most promising pupils," she explained as Bill Leafydew and Bonnie Beer tried to smile politely. "I know he will appreciate the opportunity to discuss his . . . er . . . deadly garden ideas with you in more detail."

After that the rest of us were "given things to do" (as the headmistress put it) by Miss Fairjoy.

"As well as the Carnival King and Queen floats," explained Miss Fairjoy, "we are also having a special Easter bunny float this year, and I believe the drama department are working on something *very* special." She beamed round. "I expect that by now, though, you're all wondering where you come in." (I would have been surprised if anyone had been wondering that, but I suppose there might have been one or two sad stains on the face of the earth who were.) "Well," continued Miss Fairjoy, as if she was just about to share a big secret with us, "this year, each house is to have its own float, so you will have to work together as house teams. The Thomas Paynes will be working on the daffodil montage." She pointed to a large bit of cardboard with a few yellow bits of egg box stuck on it. "DeMontforts will be doing bonnets, and the King Henrys will be working on the giant Easter bunny this session. But don't worry," she said reassuringly, "we have a rota, so you'll all have a turn. We want him to be a truly Hatton Down school bunny."

She said some other stuff about what fun it would

be (like sticking-knitting-needles-up-your-nose type fun); then everyone had to make their way to their "stations". Me and Boy Dave looked round feebly.

"What house are we again?" I asked, hoping it wasn't the King Henry the Thirds, because they get called something else.

Boy Dave shrugged. "I don't know. Yellow sort of rings a bell."

"I don't see why they bother giving us a colour and a name," I said crossly. "It would be easier to remember if it was just one or the other."

"Or nothing," pointed out Boy Dave. "I don't really want to do Easter stuff anyway."

We had started to drift slowly towards the back, ready to make a run for the door, when a disturbance went round the class.

"That's not fair!"

"Just because he's. . ."

"Tut."

*"Oh what?"*

"What's going on?" I asked Steven Longacre, who was painting an egg box the usual deathly grey-yellow of egg box daffodils.

"It's that new kid," he said in his drippy voice. "He's going to be Carnival King because his dad's lending the village all the lorries for the carnival this year."

I was quite surprised. Come to think of it, the

school probably would need a lot of lorries that year, but Tom was the last person I'd have imagined to lend them to them. We'd just assumed he was a show host or something. In any event, the last thing we'd have imagined him to be was a lorry driver.

We looked pityingly over to the front, where TC was standing staring into space next to Miss Fairjoy.

"Now," said Miss Fairjoy, who didn't seem to have noticed that she'd turned one of her class into a hate object, "Thomas . . . er . . . TC is going to come with me to try on robes. The rest of you can carry on at your work stations."

Once again, me and Boy Dave headed for the door.

We made our way to the upper field and slid down the bank at the far end, to where the stream runs and no one can see you. It was a cold day for March, and spring was still showing no signs of springing. As we sat on the grass, shivering, I started to long for summer, when we could stay there for ages catching sticklebacks in plastic cups and lazing around.

"Well, I'm not going back to make Easter bonnets," said Boy Dave stubbornly.

We'd bunked off without our coats and I tried for the tenth time to tuck my hands into my sleeves, but they pinged back up again.

"No," I agreed. By now the clouds had gone really dark grey and a bit of rain was starting to fall. "But I don't really want to stay outside either."

"Well, it'll have to be the garden centre," said Boy Dave. "There isn't anywhere else."

Where we live isn't like London – where you could disappear for years and not be seen. In our village, if you sneeze at lunch time, there's a red cross on your door by nightfall. The garden centre is a huge place just outside the village. It's about the safest place if you're bunking school, but just lately some of the staff had started giving us funny looks. That day, though, as we gazed across to the woods, grey with drizzle, we decided to risk it.

We set off over the bridge and jogged along the footpath through the trees. Some of the branches were trying to make little green shoots, but they didn't seem to be having much luck. It was hard to imagine that warm days and sun were just around the corner. I couldn't wait.

We had reached the large clearing just before the edge of the village when we hit a snag. And it was a big one. At the end of the path, where only weeks before there had been nothing but grass, there now stood a new, red-brick building.

We stopped dead. We'd forgotten all about the new community centre. It was still being built and no one was using it yet, but the problem was what it said on the notice outside: *RISE BUILDING CONTRACTORS*. Our dads!

"That's it, then," I said miserably. "Even if they don't see us, one of their blokes will for sure."

"Hang on a minute!" Boy Dave shook my arm. "I'm sure I heard. . . Yes! They had to go and finish snagging at the old mill today. Dad was moaning because they're getting paid for the whole job, not by the day. Don't you remember? They left really early to beat the traffic."

Now I came to think of it, Dad *had* gone off before anyone else was up that morning. Mum hadn't stopped going on about it for the whole of breakfast. Apparently Dad had tried to make his own tea and toast and had:

- Scraped black burned toast bits all over the kitchen
- Made the butter jammy with a dirty knife (and also black bits)
- Didn't even leave his things in the sink
- But left his teabag on the edge of the sink so that it dripped brown drops all over the floor
- Got bits of cereal stuck in the toaster (I know how he did this, though Mum doesn't. It's because he does his bread too big and it gets stuck so he has to get it out with something, which – using my super powers of deduction – must have been his cereal spoon).

And, last but NOT least:

- Made the sugar gunky with a wet spoon.

By the end of breakfast, me, Joanna and Auntie Dulcie knew his "all he had to do was make a cup of tea and a bit of toast" crimes off by heart.

From outside, the community centre looked like just a boring red-brick, cube-shaped building, but when we chanced a quick look through the door-sized gap in the wall, it was a different story. The floors were smooth and grey and had that damp, stony smell of new cement. A bit more exploring showed that the corridors, as well as going round the edges of the square, made an X-shape from corner to corner. From an aeroplane it must have looked like a box with a cross in it and little grass triangles in between. There were no stairs at all, just smooth, straight wheelchair ramps going up and down at the ends of corridors and into all the rooms. Perfect for anything with wheels.

"Wow!" said Boy Dave. "We should bring our skateboards down here."

"Yeah," I agreed, "or the bikes."

There was a short pause.

"Hmm," said Boy Dave, "slight problem."

We were both thinking the same thing – if our dads caught us, it would be like the whole record players for decks thing all over again.

By the time we'd finished looking round, it was almost lunch time, and time to head back to school. The first thing we saw when we reached the school gate was a group of kids from our class gathered round in a circle. We weren't going to bother with it at first; the sort of stuff they get excited about is mostly pretty boring, but then Ryan came over looking especially serious and pointy. It was the same look he has when he's going to go on about something scientific, but instead, he just stood looking at the other kids from our class, and for once in his life, it was as if he didn't know what to say.

In the end Boy Dave nudged him. "What?"

We were feeling really hungry by this time, and were on our way to get our packed lunches.

"Em. . ." Ryan nodded over towards the circle.

"Don't tell me they've found another pigeon," I said jokingly.

"It's TC," said Ryan at last. "Connor's decided to pick on him and everyone else is joining in."

We were really surprised.

"Why, just because he's going to be the Carnival King? No one ever wants to be it anyway."

"I think it's a bit more than that. I mean, he had that big embarrassing party and his dad was . . . well . . . like he is. And they've obviously got lots of money, so some people are jealous. Plus he's a bit . . . rounded. And also new."

Put like that, it did seem like a bit of a bad combination.

"I've been waiting for you to get back," explained Ryan. "There wasn't much I could do on my own."

Boy Dave, who had been impatiently looking over in the direction of the school (and the packed lunches), said, "We'll just go and have a bite to eat and then see if we can help."

"Mind you," I said, "if it's anything like the pigeon, he'll have died of being fed too much sweetcorn by the time we get back."

Ryan coughed. It was a particular sort of cough that meant he didn't approve. Connor used to try and pick on Ryan because he's clever and isn't the sort to get into fights. To be fair to Connor, Ryan does get away with a lot because the teachers think he's great, and putting it into teacher language, schoolwork is something Connor "struggles" with (I don't know why this should bother him particularly. Me and Boy Dave gave up the struggle years ago and haven't looked back since). Still, whatever the reasons, it was obvious that Ryan was feeling really sorry for TC.

"We'll go and quickly see what's going on," I said, "but then we're going to get our sandwiches. I'm so hungry I could eat my legs."

Sure enough, TC was right there in the middle of the group. He had his arms folded and was being pretty noncommittal, but this wasn't easy because Connor kept pushing him, knocking him off balance. There's something really nasty about watching someone being pushed like that. Our class were saying stuff like, "Yeah, fat boy, you think you're so different."

"Yeah, just because his dad has a big house."

"So no one else can be Carnival King now and you haven't even been here for ten minutes."

It was the first time I could ever remember that they'd all ganged up together to pick on one person.

Boy Dave pushed in casually next to Connor.

"Well," he said to TC, "you've got to admit that it isn't really fair. I mean, Connor really wanted to be the Carnival King himself."

Connor looked a bit confused, and this might have been because it was actually true.

Poppy Lockhart, who really wants Boy Dave to ask her out, slithered over and went in a stupid casual voice, "Hi, Dave."

He gave her an extra-dirty look. "Get lost, Poopy."

"Poor Connor," I said, "he was really looking forward to wearing those long, flowing robes, weren't you, Connor?"

Connor went red and said "NO!" really loudly.

Cal Mockford puffed out his chest. "What's it got to do with youse lot anyway?"

"And Cal had set his heart on being the Easter bunny that sits by the throne, hadn't you, Cal?" said Boy Dave.

Poppy and her silly friend Emma giggled, and so did some of the others.

"But he still can be," I pointed out. "He could wear an Easter bonnet."

Connor tried to make his two brain cells work at the same time.

"That's not the point, is it?" He was trying to look really mean because loads of people had started laughing. "That TC, he's like the rich kid, ain't he?"

Boy Dave put his hand up to his ear. "Sorry, mate, don't understand."

Connor tried again. "Well, that TC, he's . . . he thinks he's the big 'I am' just because his dad's loaded."

"Yeah," went everyone else.

"Well done, mate." I patted him on the head. "You've taught everyone to speak in pig grunts. I really think they understood you that time."

Boy Dave did an impersonation of Connor

grunting like a pig. "Grunt snuffle grunt loads of money grunt grunt."

"They won't let a pig be the Carnival King, though," I said sadly. "You'd have to be Carnival Pig."

"Yeah," said Boy Dave, "King Hog."

"Or Queen Snouty," I suggested.

Connor looked as if he wanted to smack us one, but he didn't. This isn't because we're particularly hard or good at fighting, it's just that our dads are builders and a bit big themselves (mainly their fat tummies), and there's stuff going on like Connor's dad wouldn't really like to get into a row with our dads because he sometimes does work for them.

"Anyway," said Boy Dave, "I'm a bit too hungry to be talking with you any more because it keeps making me think of sausages. TC's our mate and he's coming with us to get our sandwiches."

And so it came to be that me, Boy Dave, Ryan and TC got talking properly.

We sat on the steps by the lockers and TC told us his life story. Ryan had been right in a way – TC's family really had just come back from America (which he called the States), but they'd only been there for a bit and TC hadn't liked it much.

"I mostly played computer games," he said. "A lot of kids were seriously into it out there."

"Is that how you managed to make your dad give you all that stuff?" I asked interestedly. We'd all been wondering that – like I don't think it would matter how rich our dads were, they still wouldn't let us have half the gear that TC had.

TC nodded. "He always wants me to have the latest things so we look better than other people."

"Were all the kids in America as rich as you?" asked Ryan.

"I think there are some really poor kids in the States," said TC after a while, "but where we lived most of them were a lot richer than us, though my dad would never admit it. Take my welcome party. . ." (We coughed, but right now TC didn't need someone telling him he should definitely just call it "the party".) "It was nothing compared with what some kids out there get. One kid in my class had a skidoo party in Alaska."

We tried to imagine it. In a way it sounded great, but I wondered if it would be a bit like TC's party, where no one really enjoyed themselves. I didn't fancy being trapped out in Alaska with TC's dad.

Ryan said thoughtfully, "I suppose if they had an Alaska party, then your dad would have tried to have an Egypt party or something?"

For the first time TC almost grinned. At any rate, he made a funny long rectangle shape with his mouth.

"Exactly. It's why we had to move back to England, down here to the sticks. He lost loads of money from that sort of thing."

"But isn't your dad a truck driver?" I asked, thinking of our dads' mate Tony the Truck. I was quite sure he didn't have loads of money.

TC did the letterbox smile with his mouth again. "My dad doesn't *drive* the trucks, he owns them. It's his thing – haulage."

The penny dropped.

"And he's lending some to the village for the carnival?"

72

"Yep." TC looked suddenly gloomy again. "Everywhere we go he has to be the top guy."

"And," I said slowly, "everywhere you go you have to be the Carnival King, right?"

TC nodded miserably.

That evening at tea it was only me and Dad. Mum had left a cold chicken dinner covered in cling film on the table and a note, which said:

*Have gone to Brighton with Joanna. Tea on table. Do <u>not</u> go into the kitchen.*

Dad, who obviously didn't realize about all his crimes that morning, probably just thought she was being helpful.

We sat munching, enjoying the unusual silence for a bit. Then I asked, "Where's Auntie Dulcie?"

Auntie Dulcie isn't really my aunt as such. She's supposed to be one of Mum's relatives, but I think it's more likely that she's really a sort of elderly parasite. If we become diseased or are no longer a good food source, she will move on to a more suitable host, and may do this several times in her life cycle. She has a posh accent because she used to be an English teacher, but a lot of what she says is just gibberish, from Shakespeare and some others who are even older. I've heard they were really clever once, but I'm afraid it's mostly rambling now. Still, Dulcie obviously thinks a lot of them so no one says anything.

Anyway, the official story is that she has to live with us because she hates her own family, especially someone called Derrick.

Dad hates salad almost as much as Dulcie hates Derrick and was pulling faces like a celebrity eating an insect.

"Gone to a funeral," he said grumpily (Dulcie is always going to funerals).

After a while I asked casually, "Are you still doing the community centre thing?"

Dad stopped chewing. "Why?"

"Oh, it was just something Mum said – that I should . . . er . . . take more interest in case I ever go into the building trade myself."

He tried not to look pleased.

"Well, yer, it's getting there. We've got all the plastering done on the interior and the shell's pretty much ready for completion work."

"Mmmm." I nodded interestedly. "And I expect it'll probably have some lights soon?"

Dad looked suddenly suspicious. "Why are you asking about lights?"

"I was just thinking . . . you know . . . that they won't be able to use it for anything until it's got some lights and . . . plumbing."

Dad relaxed and accidentally ate a bit of lettuce. "That's right, mate. We'll carry on with the gennies until all the decorating's been done – maybe wire up the odd lamp – and then basically you have to think about it in order: the plumbing work would mess up the decor, so we do that. Butthenurlbelurblel ectricsblahdilaafterpaintdilaburluble."

He carried on with the boring explaining while I tried to find a good moment to ask how to make a generator work. But before I got a chance, Mum and Joanna came back.

They staggered into the living room and dumped about a hundred carrier bags on the floor. Dad immediately pulled the "disgusting salad" face again. Mum pretended she hadn't noticed.

"All right, everyone? Hello, sweetheart." She kissed the top of my head and then tried to wipe her mouth on her sleeve without me noticing. "Did you have a good day at school?"

"Yes, thank you."

She looked at me a bit oddly. "Found your dinner all right, then?"

Dad grunted and did the live insect thing. He nodded at the carrier bags. "Carry on like this, we'll be bankrupt by Christmas."

"Oh, it's just a few bits," said Mum brightly.

Joanna, who had been annoyingly eating bits of cucumber off my plate, decided that way too much time (like, at least a minute) had gone by without her being the centre of attention.

"You'll never guess," she said to Dad. "Mr Fern and Miss Robertson have suggested that I audition to be Carnival Queen. I told them I'd be really nervous, but they were, like, really supportive? And they seem to think that I've got a really good chance of being chosen?" (Joanna turns everything into a question.) "So Mum's been buying me a really gorgeous outfit to wear to the audition?"

"No need to get it all out in the living room, love," said Mum hastily, as Joanna started digging around in one of the carriers. "Let's take it upstairs and sort it out up there, shall we?" She glanced nervously at Dad.

But it would have taken one of TC's RPGs to stop her. Clothes, belts and shoes were flying everywhere. Dad goggled and then decided to try and be sarcastic.

"OH," he said in a loud, dramatic voice, "I must have made a mistake. Only I thought that this morning you all had drawers and wardrobes full of clothes upstairs. *I* thought that you had so many clothes we had no room in the house for any more. And if I remember rightly, the price of a pint down the pub with my mates is so expensive that I'm not even allowed to *sniff* one any more."

He should have learned by now that being sarcastic

to Mum and Joanna is a waste of time. Joanna said sweetly, "We're going to give my old last year's clothes to Age Concern. To help the sick?"

"And we're not just talking about one pint, are we, Dominic?" said Mum in a scary way.

Joanna pulled out a white and silver thing from one of the carriers.

"Here it is! Isn't it gorgeous? I'll go and get changed so you can all see me in it."

I stared gloomily at my chicken pieces. Dad puffed and was obviously wondering whether or not to try and stand up for himself. I don't know if it was a good or a bad thing that Dulcie chose that moment to come home from her funeral.

Dulcie always wears the same thing to funerals – a black coat with fur on the collar, and make-up. I should say that Dulcie is one of my favourite people and I wouldn't normally knock her, but when she wears make-up she looks like a severed head. She did the thing that always really annoys Dad and knocked on the front door instead of using her key.

When we heard her knocking, Mum put on a serious face and said, "That'll be Dulcie. Now please can everyone be a bit sensitive for once."

A moment later she ushered her in. "Sit down, love, it's been a trying day. Let me get you a cup of tea."

Dulcie sat down creakily. "Perhaps just a glass of water; one does feel obliged to drink so much sherry on these occasions."

Dad shuffled and looked a bit awkward. "Well . . . er . . . how was it?"

"Dom!" said Mum crossly. "It was a funeral! How do you think it was?"

"Don't worry, Angela." Dulcie waved her hand.

"Thank you, Dominic, dear; all things considered, it went very well. Although I'd forgotten quite how ghastly the Binghams are. When that dreadful Adele started reciting Tennyson through an unsanitary handkerchief, I really did think that poor Dorothy was better off out of it. Mind you," she said thoughtfully, "Dorothy wasn't exactly the sort of person you'd describe as un-ghastly. I'm not even convinced that she was very sanitary, but, of course, that may have been more in her twilight years."

I asked, "How do you mean, not very sanitary?"

Dad went, "Hrrrm."

And Mum said in a warning voice, "Jordan, Auntie Dulcie is tired."

"She was very smelly, dear," said Dulcie, "and of course Wordsworth made it worse."

Dad went "*hrmmph*" again, only louder, and Mum raised her eyebrows in a particular way.

"He took to 'going'," continued Dulcie, "wherever the fancy took him. The whole house reeked of it and one had to be very careful where one sat."

It seemed tactful to try and be grown-up about this.

"Was Wordsworth her husband?" I asked kindly.

"Oh no, dear, *Wordsworth* was a large ginger tomcat. Dorothy was absolutely devoted to him. When he died she had him stuffed."

She gazed fondly over at Nemesis, her Pekinese dog, who was dozing on Dad's armchair. Nemesis opened her eyes and gave her a disgusted look back.

"Ye-es," continued Dulcie thoughtfully, "she had it done by her dentist, but he only did it as a hobby. Regrettably, I think he must have left some of the original Wordsworth in. Really, it was like the Victorians; one had to have a pomander and smelling salts just to get through the front door."

She gave Nemesis another loving look. "I do think it's so advisable to get someone who knows what they're doing with these sorts of things."

Nemesis growled under her breath and shot Dulcie a death stare. Dad, who, unusually for him, was with Nemesis on this one, said warningly to Dulcie, "Don't even think it!" He spoiled it a bit, though, by adding, "I never wanted that flea-bitten mutt in the first place."

It's true that when Nemesis first came Dad really didn't want her. Lately, though, I had caught him stroking her a couple of times, and once I even came in and found her on his lap when he was watching telly, so I don't think he minds her too much now. Anyway, she's pretty good as long as she's in the house, and she can't bark – she just goes *mmm mmm* like that – although she does growl. She looks quite cute as well – sort of oblong with long brown fur that touches the ground and a leathery little nose, close to her eyes – like a snobby-looking Y-shape.

I should say, though, that her personality is quite a lot different from her looks, and if other dogs try to say hello to her, she quite often has "one of her moments" (as Dulcie likes to call the excessive violence that follows). Having said that, Nemesis does have one dog friend, who is Mrs White's dog, Confucius, but even that got off to a bad start. Also, she's banned from going to any events where there might be morris dancing.

I think Dulcie might have said a bit more about her friend's smelly old cat, but just then Joanna burst into the living room wearing the new outfit.

"Oh, poor Auntie." She rushed over and put her hand on Dulcie's arm. "I came as soon as I could. Was it someone you really cared for?"

It would be a mistake to think Joanna actually has real caring emotions, but she is quite good at pretending to have them because she watches a lot of those sorts of programmes on TV.

"Thank you, dear," said Dulcie coldly. "I think I can bear the grief."

Joanna put her hand on her chest. "You're so strong in yourself. It can be so hard to make the decision to move on." She shook her head sorrowfully. "I've just had to choose an outfit for the Carnival Queen auditions, and it was one of the hardest things I've ever had to do."

Normally I would have asked to leave the table, but it seemed – I don't know – somehow wrong to spoil the compassion.

We were a bit nervous about our day learning golf with Tom. The golf club is up on Chalk Hill, which is a bit behind where TC lives. You go up a long steep road to get to it, and from the ground the clubhouse looks as if it's built right at the edge of a steep white cliff. We sometimes go up there on the bikes, because the golf course has some good up-and-down bits, but the golfers can be a bit bad-tempered, and there's an old lunatic with a moustache who sometimes chases us with a stick.

The Saturday after the party we met Tom and TC at The Cedars.

"Good to see you!" said Tom, slapping the back of Boy Dave's head. "Degarriat, Smithozillo, Marconi." He did a dodge/weave that The Undertaker in WWE would have been proud of, and did some "playful" punches.

We did square smiles and went, "Er . . . ha, ha, that's us." And did our own dodge/weaves to avoid them.

Meanwhile TC stared into space and didn't seem to have particularly noticed us.

Tom happily slung his golf clubs into the boot of a brand new Land Rover.

"Can't beat the fresh air and countryside!" He took a big sniff in. "Anyone got . . . er . . . anything they need to *take care of* before we go?"

It took a moment for us to cotton on. Then Ryan said, "I'm all right for the moment, thank you," and poked me really hard in the ribs.

We piled into the Land Rover and Tom, who was obviously looking forward to the day, jumped happily into the driver's seat. He turned and gave us the thumbs up.

"A great day out on the hillside! Keep it real, that's what I say."

I think we'd always imagined the clubhouse to be much smarter than it really was, with waiters carrying little round trays and people smoking cigars in big leather armchairs. We were a bit disappointed to find out that it was just a bar with shiny fake wood tables and that the only thing that made it different was the terrible clothes.

Golf outfits aren't the only types of disgusting sports gear – some types of very tight, hideously patterned cycling things are bad, and ice skating outfits are very dire, but there is actually a point to them. The only reason for golf clothes is that some people have an unnatural longing to dress up in pink and yellow diamond jumpers with pale-blue flat caps and white trousers with plimsolls. And this is why they choose golf (because, as we discovered later, there definitely isn't any other reason for choosing it).

Tom (who had opted for pale yellow and a daring shade of green) bought us all crisps and fizzy drinks and we sat awkwardly on a table by the door while he went from table to table going, "Beddingham! Pinkers! Jimmy boy!" (whoever) "Good to see you," and attacking people in a jolly way.

After a bit, Boy Dave asked TC politely, "Do you come up here a lot, then?"

"Kind of," said TC boredly.

"Can you play golf?" I asked.

A wistful look came into TC's eyes. "Mostly on the Wii. I'm pretty good at it."

We started asking TC about what virtual games you could do. After a while, during which Tom seemed to have disappeared, me, Boy Dave and Ryan reached a telepathic agreement (with the help of bored looks and nods towards the door) to sneak out and go home. Unfortunately, just as we were about to go for the final push, the door next to us opened and a group of people streamed in.

"Tha-aat's right," said a man with a slimy voice who was holding the door open for them. "Come along in. Doormat to wipe the shoes. Yes, yes, come in. Most welcome, most welcome."

"We like to maintain the exclusivity of the club," he explained snootily. "No poor people or undesirables. We don't want to be concerned about leaving our nice cars in the car park, do we?"

The group nodded as if they completely understood.

Unfortunately, we too were having a moment of understanding.

The slimy man's large balloon tummy and the old wooden golf club he was leaning on were starting to bring back nasty memories. It was the old lunatic who sometimes chased us off the golf course. Luckily he hadn't noticed us yet.

"Listen," I whispered to TC, "we're just popping outside for a bit, OK?"

"Oh, OK," said TC, thinking we meant him as well.

I sighed, but it seemed mean to leave him behind.

"But quiet-like, yeah?" I told him sternly.

TC started to think it was like one of his games. He suddenly looked keen and a bit cleverer than he normally does,

"What do we have to watch out for?"

"The invader," hissed Boy Dave, nodding towards the stick man. "Reeeally quiet, OK?"

If this had been a film, the whole table would have tipped over or one of us would have trapped our tie in a comical way. In real life, what happened was we had almost made it out of the door when a woman in the group went, "Eeow! But you still allow children!" And they all turned and stared at us as if we were disgusting alien life forms.

The stick man stared too; then his eyes started to bulge and he let out an almighty roar.

"BOYS!" he yelled, lunging at us and trying to poke us with his stick, "OUT, OUT, BACK, BACK. AWAY!"

It was like being lions tamed by a madman. TC thought he was the best thing ever.

"Wow!" he said, staring in admiration. "How do you get past it?"

I was more worried about getting past him. His podgy body was blocking the door handle.

"You can't," I said, shoving him as hard as I could. "You . . . have to . . . escape."

"SECURITY, SECURITY," yelled the stick man.

TC sprung surprisingly into action.

"How do we access the weapons?" he demanded, looking round as if he expected to see a whole arsenal hovering somewhere. Spotting a large umbrella poking out of the coat stand, he dragged it out triumphantly like a samurai unsheathing his sword.

There was a sudden confused flailing as TC went into hand-to-hand combat against the stick man. For a second the stick man seemed to be winning, but TC, with lightning-quick reactions, grabbed another umbrella and came back dual-wielding. Luckily he seemed to think the brollies were Spartan lasers and was mostly trying to blow the stick man up rather than whack him, but it was probably just as well that a tall, thin man in a suit appeared when he did.

"Mr Whipstaff," said the thin man in a calm voice. "What seems to be the problem?" Then a bit louder, "Mr *Whipstaff*!"

TC and the stick maniac lowered their weapons.

"Ahh, Brigadier Jones!" Puffing, the stick man pulled a large white handkerchief from his pocket and wiped the sweat off his forehead. "These boys are trespassing and must be removed."

"You'd better remove yourselves, then," said the tall man to us, as if he didn't care much either way.

We were about to make a relieved bolt for it when Tom bustled out from behind the tall man as if nothing much was amiss.

"Whippers!" He banged the stick man, who we now knew was Mr Whipstaff, on the back. "Good to see you. This is my boy, TC, and his buddies Marconi, Degarriat and Smithozillo. Boys, meet Gerry Whipstaff. He manages the club here, and the Brigadier is the club treasurer."

"Whippers" did one of those crawly handshakes with Tom where they hold the arm as well. "Tom! Tom! Just the man, JUST the man! I should tell you," said Whipstaff, turning to his group, beaming, "that my dear friend Tom is very generously donating the championship cup this year. Real silver plating. Nothing but the best, eh, Tom? Ha ha. Quality, you see? None of your cheap tat."

The group turned to gaze at Tom admiringly.

"Absolutely," said Tom again, puffing out his chest and enjoying his day even more. "The Brigadier and I have just been to the safe to fetch the cup for the engraver. I've got it right here."

He plonked a large briefcase on our table and clicked it open. Inside was what looked like the FA Cup surrounded by foam.

Whipstaff's eyes gleamed. "May I?"

Carefully he squeezed the cup out of its padding and held it up to the light.

"You see?" he wheezed. "The very best quality and a most generous size. Most generous. We only have the very best here at Chalk Hill." Beads of sweaty pride were trickling down his forehead.

After that it was time for our golf lesson.

We trudged shivering behind the instructor up to what he was calling "the practice green". Apparently there're different sorts of golf club and you have to "select" the right one, but TC didn't bother. He stood in the middle of the little grass circle swinging his arms backwards and forwards madly while the instructor went, "Ahh . . . hmm . . . excellent warm up. Let's try a little bit of chipping and putting for real now, shall we?"

It was a bit difficult to explain that TC wouldn't necessarily see the need for an actual golf club, or even for any of the actual golf-type surroundings, and that his reality was more virtual to him than actual virtual reality, which he thought was real (type thing).

When the instructor finally persuaded him to let us have a go, Ryan was the only one who enjoyed it. He spent his turns going "FORE" at the top of his voice and trying to whack the ball massively.

"Just chipping and putting for now," repeated the instructor nervously.

"FORE!" yelled Ryan again. He must have got lucky, because the ball flew off at an angle and two large ladies (one of whom might have been Mrs Bagnal) threw themselves on the ground. Ryan put his hands on his hips in a satisfied way and asked the instructor what sort of handicap he thought he was.

So far as me and Boy Dave were concerned, it was the most frustrating afternoon of our lives. You end up wondering why anyone ever invented golf in the first place – like one day a deranged person said, "I know – why don't we try hitting a small ball with many different really thin sticks." And all the other deranged ones went, "Yes, that would be fun." And then they all hit themselves over the head with the sticks when they couldn't stand it any more.

In the end it started to drizzle. The instructor looked up at the sky as if he was thanking God and said, "Ahh, well," and ran for the clubhouse like a man fleeing from heavy gunfire.

Ryan was all for having another go, but me and Boy Dave said we'd rather spend a night in the bottle bank.

"We could have a go on one of those, though?" suggested Boy Dave, pointing towards the car park.

TC peered through the rain.

"You mean the Jag? I've got one of those." (He probably meant a virtual one.)

"No, those little car things."

"Golf buggies?" said TC, peering even harder.

They were looking at a line of tall oblong shapes with wheels and plastic roofs parked against the clubhouse wall.

"Yeah," said Boy Dave. "It would be a laugh – you know – like a kind of mission."

We'd realized by now that as long as we had TC with us, we could do pretty much anything and not get into trouble.

"And then what?" asked TC.

"Well, then we have to head due southwest along the main . . . er . . . hillside," said Boy Dave, trying to make it sound like a game.

"OK," said TC. "What weapons?"

I pushed over the golf bag that the instructor had left behind.

"One power stick for each player. We have to run to the buggies and drive off before. . ."

"The SWAT team arrive," finished Boy Dave.

Running was a bit of an unusual action for TC, and the best we could get out of him was a sort of trot/walk while we went, "That's it, one leg and then the other."

Ryan peered inside the first buggy. "They should be pretty simple to operate. Right. . . Hmm, I'll have to hot-wire them."

He obviously didn't have a clue. Luckily (or unluckily, as it turned out) there were quite a few with the keys still in them. In the ordinary way of things, I don't suppose people steal buggies at the golf club.

We decided that one of us would be the driver and the other would go on the roof, like a sort of buggy jousting tournament with golf clubs. Boy Dave and TC made up one team and me and Ryan were on the other. It came as a good surprise to find out that the buggies were a lot faster than they looked. TC was especially excited by this, and once he was sitting down again, he thought he was in a souped-up, indestructible, off-road mega-beast.

At Chalk Hill there are quite a few mini cliffs dotted about. They have overhanging edges, which we used to jump off on the bikes, and TC must have had a similar idea because before anyone could work out what he was doing, he chugged his buggy up to the top of one and drove over the edge.

The buggy landed with a massive wobbling thump, and Boy Dave, who had been nervously clinging to the roof, fell off. TC didn't seem to have noticed because Boy Dave just managed to roll clear before the buggy came over the cliff again. This time it landed on its nose with a massive crunch before slowly toppling over on to its back like a dying insect.

We goggled at the spinning wheels as TC crawled out of the wreckage looking a bit dazed. He made a wobbly, weaving inspection of the damage, then shook his head sadly.

"I'm going to need a fresh one."

We glanced nervously at each other. I don't think we'd ever met anyone as unrealistic as TC before.

"I'm not sure that's a good idea," I said cautiously. "We've written one off already."

"We could try turning this one back up the right way," suggested Boy Dave. "I mean," he added hopefully, "the damage might not be as bad as it looks."

As it turned out, if you didn't mind not going in a straight line, the buggy did still actually work, but we decided that for reasons of safety TC would have to drive it on his own. We took the other and chugged round for a bit, but we soon got bored.

"Come on," said Boy Dave, "let's collect TC and see if we can go home yet."

We peered out across the golf course, but the other buggy seemed to have disappeared.

"Maybe he's gone back in?" suggested Ryan.

"'Fraid not," said Boy Dave grimly.

He pointed to where a small black shape in the distance was hurtling downhill towards the fence.

Ryan frowned. "Now I come to think of it, we never did check to see whether it would stop again."

We set off as quickly as we could, bumping crazily

over the grass, but already some other people were running out of the clubhouse and TC was freewheeling really fast.

Moments later it was almost all over. TC had probably thought he was going to smash through the fence at 140 miles an hour, but, having finally stopped, he realized (given that Whippers and his stick were already on the way) the best thing would be to start again, and revved up massively. In TC's mind he was probably a gangster on a mission in a powerful getaway car. In reality, it was like a battle of wills. TC tried to drive through the fence and the fence tried not to be driven through.

The running people had almost got to him when, just in the nick of time, the posts gave way and TC was off again.

The sheep, who had, only moments before, been grazing happily on the hillside, were now trotting frantically in a long panicky line to avoid being trawled by what was basically a giant sheep net attached to the front of TC's buggy.

To make matters worse, the farmer's jeep was just appearing over the brow of the hill.

As it says in one of TC's game guides: "*Brute captains*" (read farmer) "*are tougher than their subordinates and tend to be more aggressive . . . they are more inclined to go berserk when injured. They also have access to better weaponry than other brutes*." As far as TC was concerned, it was the "dead man's click".

"Do you think we should try and do something?" I asked, as we beat a hasty retreat.

"Too late." Boy Dave shook his head. "He's smoked."

Slowly we wandered back down to the village. It was probably going to be best to lie low for a while.

I should say at this point that if by "lie low" we had meant hide in a mountain network of secret tunnels for a few years, moving only at night, with no radio contact of any kind, that might just about have done it.

We'd thought before that TC's dad had something seriously wrong with him, but what he did next just went to prove it: he came round our houses and tried to have a "man to man" chat with our dads.

When I got home that evening Dad was *fuming*. Tom had given him the sort of talk he had given Ryan – how he knew we were TC's buddies and, heck, he didn't know how we did things in our own homes but wasn't it time that Dad taught me some basic rights from wrongs. And TC was a decent kid but some people took advantage of his kind heart . . . la, la, etc.

I'd never seen my dad like that before. He's normally a grumpy, miserable sort of person who says, "Well, you'll have to pay for it, and no more pocket money until you do." And generally thinks up punishments or keeps mentioning things in an annoying way. Sometimes he goes bright red and shouts, but he normally stomps off down the pub way before that happens.

That evening, though (for reasons that no one really understood, but might have been that he was determined not to give Nemesis the chance to sit on it), he refused to get out of his armchair. Instead he sat there ranting like a demented king on a saggy throne.

"That PILLOCK! Coming round here! Sitting in

MY living room! Telling me how to raise MY kid! Do you know what he said? EH? Do you know what he said? He said that if money was the problem he'd be only too happy to write me a cheque so that I could get Jordan some decent clothes. There's nothing WRONG WITH MY SON'S CLOTHES! It's his HEAD that's got something wrong with it."

There was no point trying to put the telly on, and I think we were all a bit scared to try and leave the room in case it set him off worse. Instead we sat round trying to be sympathetic and calm him down. Mum was on the arm of the sofa with me beside her, Joanna was sprawled across the kitchen table and Dulcie was doing the crossword on the other comfy chair. Nemesis, who normally likes to sit on Dad's chair, and obviously thought he'd been sitting in it far too long, was eyeballing him from the safe distance of the fireplace.

I thought Dad's remark about my head being a problem was a bit offensive actually, so when he finally breathed in I said, "In case you hadn't noticed, it wasn't actually us that did anything, it was TC. He was the one who went into the fence."

"And what kind of a stupid name is that?" yelled Dad, who obviously wasn't in the mood to have a conversation in the right order.

"I suppose you think calling him Thomas would be better, do you?" I asked sarcastically.

Dad jabbed his finger at me. "ALL YOU HAD TO DO WAS LAST A HALF A DAY AT THAT ********* GOLF COURSE WITHOUT WRECKING THE JOINT AND YOU COULDN'T EVEN DO THAT!"

"IT WASN'T MY FAULT!" I yelled back. "It was that TC. He. . ." I struggled to find a way to say it. "He doesn't understand about real life."

Mum put a hand on my shoulder. "Dom? Don't you think you should hear what he's got to say?"

But it was another five minutes before I could get a word in edgeways.

I'd just started to explain about how Tom didn't understand that everything that had happened was what TC had told us to do, and how we'd thought it was all right because his dad seemed to be, like, the big man up there, when the phone rang.

"If that's Big Dave," Mum said sternly to Dad, "you're not allowed to speak to him until you've calmed down. I'm surprised Shelley let him ring."

But as it turned out, it was Ryan's mum.

This was very unusual. Ryan's mum is incredibly dozy and normally only interested in her art things. The last time she rang our house was years ago when Ryan had managed to get to the airport on his own and board a plane. And even then, by the time she actually called, Ryan was being escorted back from Colombia by armed guards in dark glasses.

Mum came back and I could tell her sympathetic mood had changed somewhat.

"What's all this about Ryan's family having some sort of embarrassing disease?"

It was one of those tones of voice which used to mean Santa was about to get a letter saying I hadn't been good.

Over the next few weeks the weather got better and the paths around the village stopped being frosty and turned to mud. We didn't mind; it meant spring was finally on the way. The trees and fields were getting greener every day and there had even been a few times lately where a brand-new shiny sun had blinked through the clouds. Most spring-like of all, though, was Andy getting his boats out of the shed for the first time that year. As soon as the mornings got a bit lighter we'd be able to plan an early morning row down the stream (this has to be early morning so we can get the boat back before Andy gets up).

Meanwhile, and a lot less excitingly, the different houses in the school went float crazy. The school had decided to give a prize to whichever house did the best float.

"First prize," announced Miss Fairjoy that Monday, "will be a book token each and fifty bonus points for the winning house." Miss Fairjoy is a thin and pale drippy sort of person with long, straggly blonde hair, but today her normally sleepy eyes had a fanatical mad gleam. "The greatest achievement will be when the school romps home with the Easter Parade Cup!" Unusually hearty, she punched the air. "But we're up against stiff opposition. The young farmers have the advantage of a range of live animals on their float – but this could go also go against them. Then there's the junior St John Ambulance and the youth group from the church. However, our biggest threat comes from the Girl Guides. I've heard their new captain is determined and ruthless." She gave us the sort of look that normally goes with banging your fist on a table. "Our floats must be stunning, our costumes amazing and our Easter rabbit spectacular. We must go into that parade as if our lives depended on it. Bonnie Beer and Bill Leafydew must be dazzled and delighted. I need that garden party and I'm relying on you – each and every one of you – to go out there and bring it home!"

"Hooray!" went our pathetic class.

Steven Longacre rubbed his hands together gleefully. Poppy and Emma waved their arms and went "Eeeee." Lin Maize stared determinedly from black-dot eyes. Some kids (including Connor and Cal) hung on to each other and jumped up and down; others clapped.

All I could think was that some people are just mad for the opportunity to win. It doesn't matter what they win – it could be anything – like you could say to our class: *And the winning float will have the once-in-a-lifetime chance to*:

- Stick a woodlouse up their nose.
- Poke a pencil in their ears.
- Go paddling in the sewers.

And they'd all look at each other excitedly and cheer and have arguments in the yard:

"We're going to win!"

"No way!"

Until the big day when the winning team could wave their woodlice, pencils, and sewer tokens in the other teams' faces and go, "Lose-ers!"

Our class became crazed by dreams of victory. The Thomas Paynes' daffodil monta-strosity for the spring animals got huger and huger until the wall of the school gym looked as if it was covered in lumpy, yellowish mould. The DeMontforts' Easter bonnets became huge floppy head-gardens, and Poppy and Emma finished their bunny outfits for the King Henrys and started wearing them as often as they could.

This was especially annoying because Poppy seemed to think that when Boy Dave saw her dressed up as a rabbit he would suddenly realize how cute and fluffy she was and beg her to go out with him.

She and Emma kept coming up to us and wiffling their noses and pretending to wash their ears. Obviously we said, "Get lost, rat-girls" and other stuff, but it didn't help.

Meanwhile, in the middle of all the crazed activity, the giant Easter bunny smiled with big cheery eyes as giant lumpy Easter eggs appeared around him as fast as the papier mâchè dried on the balloons. It was as if he was laying them sneakily like a hen in the hope of creating a spotty, zigzagged rabbit force that would eventually mutate and rule the universe.

That Thursday we were clearing up at the end of a particularly grim session of crêpe paper flower-making when I asked Boy Dave, "Coming to youth club tonight?"

The youth club takes place on Tuesdays and Thursdays in the village hall and is run by volunteer grown-ups who hide behind the sweet bar and moan about how they've had to do more nights than anyone else. There's a lumpy pool table and a table-tennis table which doesn't fit together properly in the middle any more. In summer we don't normally bother with Thursday youth club because it's seniors' night and the older ones don't let you near the pool table. In winter, though, it gets so dark in the village it's about the only place you can go, so it was one of those questions I thought I knew the answer to.

Except that Boy Dave coughed and said, "I . . . er . . . can't tonight." He was gaze-avoiding me and I noticed that he had gone a bit red. "I would normally. It's just that I . . . promised TC I'd meet him after school to play some computer games."

I stared. "After all that's happened?"

"That wasn't exactly his fault," pointed out Boy Dave. "And he still really wants to be our friend."

"But it wasn't exactly *not* his fault either," I also pointed out. "That TC – I mean, he's. . ." I tried to think of a good way to put it. In the end I gave up and finished lamely, "You've seen what his dad's like."

"He can't help that, can he?" said Boy Dave, "I mean – look at ours. And there'll probably never be another chance like it. No one else we know has all that brilliant stuff, and it's not like we're ever going to get it."

For a few moments we carried on cramming things into the art cupboard in silence. And it was an awkward silence of the sort that me and Boy Dave hardly ever have.

After a bit Boy Dave said, "Look, why don't you come as well? I'd kind of meant to mention it earlier, but then other stuff came up and I forgot. I know TC meant you could come as well."

I wasn't sure that I wanted to spend an evening round TC's, but I didn't want Boy Dave to think I was being mean.

"OK," I said slowly, "but not for long."

"Sure. Just an hour or so, yeah?"

Looking back on it, I should have realized it was weird – the way he looked so relieved.

\*

TC met us by the gates and as we started slowly up the hill (TC goes very slowly), I had an uneasy feeling. Something about The Cedars, even more now TC's family lived there, gave me the creeps – maybe it was all those perfect un-lived-in rooms. One thing was for sure – I definitely wasn't looking forward to seeing Tom again.

We went in through the back to the kitchen. On the table were microwave burgers and chips, a large bottle of cherryade and some brown-looking cut-up apples. TC looked at them disgustedly.

"My mum said Isabelle has to make fruit, but I don't really enjoy fruit. We can throw it away."

"Who's Isabelle?" I asked.

"She's French. I think she's meant to look after me and Davina."

We were doing our microwave burger "snack" when Isabelle came in. She was about the same age as Boy Dave's brother, Craig (21), and was skinny, with short, dyed bright-red hair.

"You have found the food," she told TC, giving us a dirty look. "Don't make mess."

"We can take these up," said TC, when she had gone, "and eat while we're playing."

It was like being in a timeless food- and cherryade-filled world. Even though it was only just getting dark outside anyway, TC drew the curtains.

"It's Isabelle," he explained, depressedly. "She opens them."

We chose our games by the light of a small table lamp and finished the burgers and chips while we played. TC's mum had bought him some cereal bars as part of his "healthy diet", so we ate about ten of those for afters, followed by a few bags of crisps.

I started to realize why this sort of thing is good for gamers – you get a weird sort of sitting-down energy – like actual running around would make you sick, but you could play the games for ages.

After a few hours, though, I felt achy from sitting down too long and was starting to get that feeling you get at Christmas when you've eaten the whole chocolate stocking, Christmas dinner, Christmas pudding and a mince pie and cream (even though you don't really like them), and the house is stuffy and you haven't been out yet. It was a bit of a shock when Isabelle poked her head round the door and said, "You come for your tea now."

She switched on the main light and TC howled as if the brightness burned his eyes.

I stared at all the wrappers and cans strewn everywhere. It seemed impossible that three people could have eaten and drunk so much. Isabelle disappeared back downstairs and I got out my mobile to check the time. It was gone seven. We'd been playing for almost three and a half hours.

"My mum's going to be mad," I said.

"And mine," said Boy Dave.

We eat quite early in our houses because our dads start work at seven-thirty in the morning and by the time they get home they're starving.

"I think you might be invited to tea," said TC gloomily.

The thought of trying to eat anything else made me feel a bit anxious, and I was just about to say thanks but no thanks, when the door opened again. It was Tom.

"So this is where you're hiding." He strode over, pretended to shake hands, then slapped our shoulders. "Degarriat, Smithozillo, how's life treating you?" He seemed to have forgotten that our dads had already told him our real names.

"OK," we ventured, not sure if we should try to seem a bit miserable after the problems at the golf club. Luckily Tom seemed to have made up what really happened afterwards into what he thought *should* have happened. (Grown-ups quite often do this. My dad and Big Dave are always telling stories about things that have happened as if they were really funny and they both thought it was a big laugh even when really, at the time, they were completely grumpy and didn't see the funny side at all.) In Tom's mind, our dads probably thought he was a great guy and were grateful to him for his advice and me and Boy Dave had seen the error of our ways (and were probably now calling our dads "sir" and other American good-behaviour-type stuff).

"So glad you came round this afternoon," said Tom, as if we'd come to see the whole family. "And a big WD for taking responsibility for your mistake the other day." He biffed TC over the back of his head. "Good to see you with your new buddies. Come on down; Bosie's dying to meet you two crazy characters again. She's prepared something really special."

Normally we would have made an excuse to get out of it, but there was something about Tom that made you think that it would just go horribly wrong – like if we said our mums wanted us back, he'd ring them and tell them we had to stay. If we said we couldn't manage anything else, he'd say we only had to eat a little bit, and so on. It got to the point where, whatever excuse I could think of, I knew Tom would find a way round it.

Dismally we followed him down all the stairs to the dining room, where TC's mum was tossing salad in a huge bowl with two big spoons. Tom seemed to be waiting for her to finish before we sat down, so we all stood and watched politely.

It was like clothes in a washing machine: up and down went the lettuce, round and round. I started to wonder if it would ever end. Tom stood there smiling his white smile while me and Boy Dave fidgeted and flicked the odd nervous glance at each other. TC glazed over. On and on went the salad-tossing, like some sort of voodoo where TC's mum had gone into a trance to cast out demons. I wouldn't have been surprised if she'd started chanting.

After what seemed like half an hour, Isabelle came in with some plates. She didn't seem to notice there was a ritual going on and banged them down loudly on the table.

"They make mess," she told TC's mum, as soon as she saw us. "I say to them not to make mess and they make mess."

TC's mum pretended not to hear.

"Hi." She gave us a gleaming smile as if we'd only just come in. "Take a seat."

When my mum does tea, she brings plates out one at a time with food already on them and plonks them bad-temperedly in front of us. Unless she's actually going out, she's mostly a bit scruffy in denim skirts or jeans and T-shirts. TC's mum was as perfect-looking as she had been at the party. Her yellow hair was so neat it looked like a wig, and her shirt and skirt still had ironing creases. What with her weird orangey-brown suntan I got to thinking that she was a bit virtual-looking herself.

The table looked like a picture in a magazine, with white flowers in the middle, a bright white cloth, table mats, water glasses and sparkling knives and forks. It wasn't really the sort of table you could actually eat at.

To make things even weirder, Boy Dave's chair had a pile of cushions on it, so he ended up being quite a bit higher than me.

"Mmm," said Tom, taking a seat at the head, "this looks great."

TC's mum rested her hand on her chin and gave us a little smile. "Salad?"

"Yes, thank you," we said politely.

"Isabelle," said TC's mum, "help them to salad."

Isabelle gave us a rude look and plonked a couple of lumps of lettuce and tomatoes on our plates.

"Water?" said TC's mum. "Juice?"

"Em . . . yes, thank you," we said again.

"Isabelle," said TC's mum, "help them to drinks."

Isabelle sloshed some water into our glasses from a jug.

Tom, who had been screwing loads of pepper and salt on his salad, shovelled in a huge mouthful and started chewing like the close-up in an advert where the person is meant to be really enjoying his meal.

"So," he said through the delicious mouthful, "tell me about yourselves."

I started to wonder if we could pretend to be taken ill. I thought about pretending to choke, but I wouldn't have put it past Tom to do mouth-to-mouth resuscitation.

"We . . . er . . . enjoy sport," I said nervously.

"Good," said Tom, "and what else?"

I racked my brains.

"Playing for the team."

"Excellent," said Tom, "and what else?"

"Barbecues and golf?" suggested Boy Dave.

Tom clicked his fingers, pointed at Boy Dave and winked.

"Can't beat it! What are your hobbies?"

It was like torture – ask enough questions and they're bound to give themselves away. Normally I expect we could have thought up quite a few hobbies, but we'd already used most of them up in the "enjoy" section.

"Stuffing animals?" I suggested after a bit, thinking of Dulcie's friend's dentist.

There was a bit of a silence.

"Bosie's taken up yoga," said Tom in such a way as to suggest that yoga was a proper sort of hobby.

"Yes, we do a bit of that," said Boy Dave hastily. "More than the stuffing, actually."

TC's mum looked interested. "Don't you find it's great for centring yourself?" she asked. "I think it's such a good way to just touch base."

I should say at this point that me and Boy Dave weren't really sure what yoga was. Our mums had gone a couple of times but they said it made them feel too laid back to get on with anything afterwards. I'd always thought it was some sort of group nap but TC's mum made it sound like baseball. At the end of the day it didn't matter as long as she carried on talking and we didn't have to answer any more questions.

"I'm sensitive to the supernatural," explained TC's mum, enjoying all our interested nodding. "So it's very important for me to relax. I'm the seventh child of a seventh child. . ."

"Youngest of two, sweetness," corrected Tom.

TC's mum ignored him.

"And second sight runs in my family. My mother – and her mother before her – passed it down to me, but it can be a burden as well as a gift. Spirits surround me at all times. They talk in their wispy voices. . ."

"All that bending about," said Tom, desperately

trying to get back to the yoga. "That'll do you good."

"As long as I'm careful," agreed TC's mum, "not to let bad spirits enter my body when I'm in a state of spiritual openess."

TC, who had also been starting dreamily into space – but was probably thinking more of his spirit entering a computer – said, "It's this sort of stuff that got you kicked out of the 'swap kids 'n' swim club'."

Tom squirmed. "Bosie just felt that some of those kids weren't the right sort of friends for Davina, didn't you, dear?"

"And some folk have very closed minds," said TC's mum.

She would have carried on, but at that moment Davina (who, let's face it, might be another reason why they kicked Bosie out of the swapping kids club) made her entrance. Today she was dressed as the troll version of Snow White.

"MY COOSHUNS!" she shrieked, storming over to Boy Dave and trying to push him off his chair. "GET OFF, POO-POO HEAD!"

Boy Dave stared at her and then seized his chance. "Yes, I probably had better be going."

Tom and TC's mum laughed.

"You're sitting on her cushions," explained TC's mum as Troll White clawed at Boy Dave's legs. "Davina, dear, please talk politely to our guests."

Davina grabbed a cushion and tried to yank it out from underneath Boy Dave's bottom.

"GET YOUR STINKY POO BUM OFF."

"Isabelle," said TC's mum, "Davina wants some more cushions."

"NO," yelled Davina, "I WANT THESE COOSHUNS. THESE ARE MY COOSHUNS AND HE CAN'T SIT ON THEM BECAUSE HE IS A BIG PLOPPY STINK PANTS."

Isabelle said, "She wants those cushions."

"So," said Tom to us as Boy Dave, not sure whether he was allowed to get off or not, lurched like a boat in a storm and tried to bat Davina out the way, "tell me about your families."

I could go on and tell you all about tea at TC's, but it just went on like that, really. In the end Boy Dave had to move, and Davina said she would only eat Coco Pops. TC said he didn't enjoy salad and also had Coco Pops but with cherryade instead of milk. Me and Boy Dave told Tom that our dads liked sports, barbecues and golf and Tom said they should come up to the club sometime, which made us feel nervous. Finally Isabelle piled all the things into the middle of the table by way of clearing them up and we said we'd better be going.

Tom saw us off at the door.

"See you, fellas." He slapped our backs. "Keep it real."

We walked down the long driveway feeling burpy and a bit sick.

"It's a shame we can't just go there and play the games without having to talk to his mum and dad," said Boy Dave.

I didn't say anything. My eyes were dry and sore and I was still trying really hard not to imagine any kind of food in case it made the sickness worse. So far as I was concerned, it wasn't a shame at all.

I should have realized then that there was something wrong – but I didn't. By the time I did realize, it was too late.

As we neared the middle of March, I was getting completely sick of the Easter Parade. Obviously Joanna had been chosen as Carnival Queen and the whole of our house had been turned into a shrine of worship for her outfit. Mum was meant to be making it but she's not very good at sewing so she had to keep asking Dulcie, who made a big fuss about helping and tried to do completely different things from what Mum wanted.

"I don't mind helping, Angela dear," she kept saying, "but I really don't see why Joanna can't just wear a nice frock from M&S."

As far as Dulcie is concerned, M&S is the answer to all clothes problems, and I have many uncool jumpers to prove it.

Then Mum would say something like, "Since when did M&S start doing queen outfits?"

And then they'd end up having an argument and Joanna would go upstairs and cry – but with a real handkerchief, so everyone could see her dabbing her eyes.

By now me and Dad were banned from going anywhere except the television area, and had to eat our tea on the settee because the material and sewing machine were permanently laid out on the table. We moaned a lot about this, but secretly we'd got some quite nice little habits going, like eating dinner in front of the telly. We'd even managed to agree on the TV planner.

The last lesson that Tuesday was science, which, obviously, Ryan loves, but me and Boy Dave don't normally enjoy. Still, even Miss Stormberry couldn't turn science into anything to do with the Easter Parade.

The nights were getting shorter now and that afternoon had the sharp, clean smell of spring. After spending Monday night in with Dad and the queen outfit arguments, I was desperate to get out.

"You coming to juniors tonight?" I whispered to Boy Dave. "We could have a game of pool."

Boy Dave was busy flicking bits of chewed paper at the back of Steven Longacre's head, and there was a bit of a pause.

"Actually. . ." He tried to sound casual. "I've arranged for us to go over to TC's tonight and do some games again."

My mouth fell open so wide that my jaw almost hit the desk.

"What about Tom? What if they make you stay to tea? What about the troll?"

"It's not the problem we thought it was. TC says they only do it if he has friends round because Tom and Bosie want to show what a nice family they are. Normally he just does his own thing and has snacks in his room. He's not going to tell them we're coming this time, so we can sneak upstairs and play the games and they'll never even know we're there."

I frowned. It wasn't that I didn't like the games, exactly. In other circumstances, I probably wouldn't have minded, but there was something about TC's dark den that made me feel really closed in. I didn't like the way there was absolutely no daylight, and the smell of old burgers and all that sick-making food you seemed to eat without knowing. *They'll never even know we're there.* Boy Dave hadn't meant to, but he'd made it sound like rotting away in a dungeon.

"I don't want to spend another evening stuck in," I told him firmly. "Let's just go to youth club – yeah?"

But instead of going, "Oh, OK, then" like I would have expected, Boy Dave looked blank in a way that was creepily like TC.

"I've said I'll go now." He nudged me. "Come on. You can have a go on the Wii."

I stared down to the front of the class, where Ryan was bent over a test tube filling it up with some green liquid while Miss Robertson, the science teacher, looked on dotingly.

"I think. . ." I stopped. "Actually, I think I'll just ask Ryan if he's coming out instead."

I'd hoped that Boy Dave wouldn't want to go on his own. But he just shrugged and looked away.

For the whole rest of the lesson, I couldn't stop thinking about it. It should have been no big deal, but I stared angrily at the back of TC's head and wished he'd never even moved to our village. In a way it wasn't fair. After all, he'd only been trying to make friends – but if he wanted to be friends, why couldn't he ask to come out with us? Why did he have to get people back to his nasty little pit all the time like a podgy spider in its stinky web?

It felt weird that evening, walking home on my own. I'd agreed to meet Ryan later on, and our friends Daisy and Claire were going to youth club as well, so it wasn't as if I wouldn't have anyone to hang round with.

But that didn't change the fact that it had been really strange seeing Boy Dave go off up the hill with TC. They were talking and waving their hands around, discussing the games already. I knew it was the games, because TC wouldn't get so excited about anything else.

The next day Boy Dave had to help his dad make a barbecue, and on Thursday evening at youth club he never showed up either. I'd arranged to meet him at Hangman's Lane and thought maybe he'd gone on ahead or was running late, but by the time eight-thirty had come and gone and his phone had gone over to message, I started to think there was something wrong.

"Do you think I should ring his dad?" I asked Ryan.

We were walking up the road to the graveyard.

Ryan was quiet for a bit, which isn't like him. "I suppose you could."

"I mean, he might have had an accident. It's pretty dark down the lane."

Ryan gave me a bit of a look. "Not very likely, though, is it?"

We didn't talk again until we were sitting on one of the big tombs in the graveyard. In the moonlight the church looked soft and unreal, as if it were made of clay.

"I think, em. . ." Ryan said at last. He paused. "I think he's actually round at TC's."

While I took this in I looked up at the black raggedy shapes of the crows' nests, high in the bare branches of the trees. I supposed they were all up there, hunkered down for the night, and for some reason I felt jealous of them being so cosy.

"He can't be. He wouldn't have agreed to meet me otherwise." But inside I wasn't so sure.

"I expect he only meant to go there for a little while," said Ryan, and it was obvious he was trying to make me feel better. "But then got into one of the games and forgot the time. It's easy to do. I'm the same with my inventions."

"He didn't go round there after school."

"No," agreed Ryan thoughtfully. "But I think he did go afterwards. Maybe he didn't want you to know. He gets embarrassed, because he knows you don't approve."

Come to think of it, there had been quite a few times that week when Boy Dave had made excuses not to meet up. On Saturday he'd said his mum wanted him to wait in because Craig was coming round. And he'd gone home early on Sunday. Then Monday and yesterday. I'd thought it was a bit weird, but it hadn't been that long since all the problems at the golf course – I'd just supposed he wanted to keep the peace.

"Oh well," I tried not to let on. "We'll see him tomorrow. What shall we do now?"

We spent some time altering the notices on the board inside the entrance to the church to annoy the vicar – like, Women's Institute needs potty pants (instead of potted plants) and then spent the rest of the evening playing Death or Glory with Claire and Daisy. This is a game Ryan invented which has complicated rules to do with different parts of the graveyard. Like a Tovey-Parsons is where you have to run from the grave of William Tovey to the grave of Pamela Parsons, and so on. Unless you were actually there when it got invented, you'd find it really hard to learn, and we don't always stick to the rules anyway.

Actually, the evening didn't turn out too bad. It was me and Claire against Ryan and Daisy. I don't really see the point in going out with girls, but if I did, I'd choose Claire. She's got long, wild, orangey hair and is one of those people who's always happy. Also, she's not at all girly or stupid – like she just wears jeans and T-shirts and doesn't mind running around and getting dirty. She and Daisy are both pretty good like that, not like the girls from our school.

They don't normally hang out with us on seniors' night, because they prefer to hang round the older boys. I don't know why they did this time, but I was glad they had. We won, by the way. Claire can run almost as fast as me and I'm the fastest runner I know.

At the end of the evening we bought some fizzy drinks from the kiosk in the youth club and walked back down past the end of Hangman's Lane and across the edge of the village green. We normally say goodbye to Boy Dave at Hangman's Lane, and it felt strange not watching his torch bob away through the trees. With a twinge of embarrassment, I realized that Claire was looking at me.

"Where is he tonight, anyway?"

"Busy, I s'pose."

There was a bit of a silence.

"You're different when you're not with him."

It wasn't meant to be harsh, but it felt it. I looked at the ground. OK, so I was different, what did she expect me to do about it? Just because he was my best mate didn't mean I could make him hang round with me.

Claire grinned. "What I mean is – you're a lot easier to talk to when the BD's not around." (Which is what she and Daisy sometimes call Boy Dave.)

Then she started telling me a funny story about her rugby team getting pulverized by the Girl Guides' rugby team, who were just like the New Zealand All Blacks.

I felt happy as I walked up the garden path that night – as if all my worries had been silly and over the top. But over the next few weeks, everything took a nosedive.

Ryan was working on something "top secret" and didn't want to go out much, and Boy Dave and TC had started spending every break time together, sitting in a corner of the schoolyard playing Nintendo DS and having long, boring conversations about the games. I tried sitting with them, but it had got to the point where I didn't understand what they were talking about most of the time. Almost every day after school, they disappeared up the hill to TC's.

The ground was spreading with purple and yellow flowers now, and everywhere you looked birds were speeding by with twigs in their beaks. But, whereas I'd been looking forward to football and boating and trips to the sea on the train, the thought made me feel strange now.

If I'm honest, I think I was feeling something that I hardly ever feel. I was feeling sad.

It wasn't as if me and Boy Dave had fallen out or had an argument. In a way it might have been better if we had; at least we could have made it up. Instead, it was just like two boats gradually gliding apart on a pond, too far out to reach them or change anything.

Me and Ryan took to spending more time together. But, up until then, Ryan had preferred to do his own thing and join in with me and Boy Dave when it suited him. There were quite a few times now when he went to the school library at lunch time to look something up on the internet and, although he didn't say it, I got the feeling that I was cramping his style. When I wasn't at school, I took to staying in a lot, watching telly downstairs at home.

One Saturday evening towards the end of March, we were in the middle of an especially dull episode of *ER* when Dad said in a way that was meant to sound casual, "Not going out tonight, Jordan?"

I'd had the feeling he had been building up to asking me something like this for a while, but I wished he hadn't.

"I thought I'd stay in."

Mum said, "That's not indigestion, that's a heart attack."

Joanna was out, so she and Dulcie had dared to have a rest from the queen outfit and were watching with us.

"You and the Boy fallen out, have you?" asked Dad, trying to make it sound as if he was just making conversation.

I felt myself go red. How was I supposed to explain

that nowadays Boy Dave preferred computer games to doing anything real, including anything so obviously boring as hanging out with me?

We carried on watching telly for a bit, and I was just going to go and hide upstairs when Dad said briskly, "Come on, Jordie, get your shoes. I'm taking you down the Black Horse for a game of pool. Ange?" he said loudly. "I'm taking him down the Black Horse."

Mum nodded knowingly and said, "I knew it! Appendicitis, and she's going to turn out to be his daughter."

The Black Horse is the local pub. It has beams on the ceiling and brass horseshoes on the pillars. There are tatty green velvet chairs and stools, and red wallpaper. The pictures are of hunting people with horses and dogs. Our dads like the back bar, where all the old boys sit in a line on exactly the same stool every night. It has a pool room with a long overhead light and a fringed lampshade.

The evenings were still a bit chilly for outside, so Dad bought me orange and crisps and a pint for himself, then we sat in the back bar to wait for the pool table to be free.

"School going all right?" he asked after a bit.

"Fine."

I don't often really look at my dad. I suppose he looks just like you'd think a builder would look. His work clothes are old ripped jeans over tracksuits, with big orange boots and a red padded check jacket and hardhat. He doesn't look much different at home, except he wears trackies without the jeans and a bit cleaner T-shirts. The only time he and Big

Dave ever dress up smartly is if they're going to see about a big job. Then it's suits and ties, but they find them uncomfortable and it shows.

Sitting opposite him now, it was hard not to notice his dusty, up-on-end hair and the sort of face that's been out in all weather. For once he was looking at me a bit kindly.

"What's going on with you and the Boy?"

I felt my crisps go sticky in my mouth.

"Had an argument?" he asked sternly.

"No."

There was silence, and Dad sipped his pint thoughtfully.

"Spending a lot of time with the rich kid, is he?"

I tried not to stare. How could he know? Dad must have guessed what I was thinking because he said, "I saw him when I went round to collect Big Dave the other day – hardly recognized the kid. Big Dave tells me he's up The Cedars most nights."

I nodded and Dad said, "Filled out a bit, hasn't he?"

It was a bit hard to imagine how my dad, of all people, could have the cheek to say that. But he was right; Boy Dave had been changing shape lately. In fact, from behind, it was hard to tell him and TC apart.

Dad leaned back in his chair and pulled a serious face.

"You shouldn't take it to heart so much. You and the Boy go back for ever. Your mums only just shaved past each other in the hospital when you were born. It's the same with me and his dad – we go back a long, long way. But I'll tell you this, you can't have a friendship that lasts for forty years and have it always be exactly how you want it to be. Right? What you've got to remember is that having a mate like him is worth an awful lot more than a few hiccups along the way."

I swallowed. How could I explain that Boy Dave didn't see the *point* in being my friend any more?

"And for *him*, having a mate like *you* is worth an awful lot too," Dad continued. "All what's going on now won't last. And when it does pass over, what's going to be left, eh? *Your* friendship, that's what." Dad chuckled. "I'll tell you something, though; whatever he's doing isn't suiting him. If I were you, I'd try and shake him out of it before people start mistaking him for a beach ball."

This is the sort of joke that Dad and Big Dave find hilarious and we mostly don't. As Dad roared with laughter, I started to wonder if he'd looked at his own tummy lately. Still, he must have said something right because I started to feel a bit better inside.

That would have been the end of anything worth mentioning about that particular evening, except for a weird thing that happened a few moments later.

Me and Dad were having one of those awkward silences that normally leads to a discussion about football when a grumpy old boy called Issiah shouted "Hoi" really loudly from the pool room. The next thing we knew a young man with greasy-looking blond hair charged out of the doorway.

My dad, not being as quick-thinking as everyone seemed to suppose afterwards, accidentally stuck his leg out at exactly the same time as the greasy-haired young man ran past, and he went sprawling face down on the floor. Dad got up to help him but people started shouting.

"That's it. Hold on to him, Dom. Don't let him get away."

And a handful of blokes, including Andy, the landlord, barged over and yanked the young man to his feet. Issiah reached into one of the young man's pockets and pulled out a handful of fifty-pence pieces. Very deliberately, he started to count them out: "Fifty, one pound, one pound fifty. . ."

Dad grabbed hold of my arm to drag me out of the way, but then let go and sat looking at the young man with an expression that I couldn't make out. I suppose it was Dad looking so hard that made me look as well. And that was when I realized who he was. There wasn't any reason not to just say it, but something in the way they were all stood round made me lean over and whisper to Dad.

"That's Craig's friend."

When he was younger and still lived at home, me and Boy Dave used to really look up to Craig and his mates. The greasy-haired young man had been younger then, but I still recognized him. He'd been the only one who wasn't really sarcastic to us when we tried to hang out with them. His name was something like chewing gum. . .

"Chiggley," I hissed to Dad. "His name's Chiggley."

"Shh," said Dad grimly, "don't shout it out for all to hear."

I should say that I still didn't know why everyone was being so weird, but over the next few minutes it dawned on me. In our village there's hardly any crime and mostly everyone trusts everyone else – so if you want a game of pool, you stick a couple of fifty-pence pieces on the pool table; then someone comes and tells you when it's your turn. But tonight the pool money had ended up in Chiggley's pocket.

"Three pounds fifty," said Issiah, his rubbery face twitching as he finished counting. "Three and a half lousy quid." He looked into Chiggley's pale eyes. "Your father would die for shame."

I thought maybe Andy, Issiah and the others would get PC White, but they didn't. They just slung Chiggley out of the door and told him to never come back. In our village this is a pretty big deal, seeing as there's only one pub.

I wanted to talk about it, but for some reason Dad didn't. All he would say was that it was the farmhand Ray Chiggley's son and that they wouldn't call PC White out of respect for him.

The pool table came free not long after, and me and Dad had one of those games where Dad gives instructions like, "Slide it off the top, son," which don't really mean anything if you try and turn them into real actions.

Over the next few days I forgot all about Chiggley. I was too busy thinking about Dad's advice (the friendship thing, not the pool tips). It was all very well to talk about shaking Boy Dave out of the big house, but it just wasn't that easy. I'd already tried to persuade him to come out some evenings, but we'd never done anything particular anyway. Most of the time we'd just got together and made it up as we went along. So nowadays the conversation always ended up being the same.

"Are you out tonight?"

"Why? What's happening?"

"Dunno. I just thought . . . you might be out and about, that's all."

I mean, what can you say – table tennis at the youth club? Football on the green? Except that compared with being whatever team you want in the FIFA cup finals, it sounds pathetic.

"Maybe." Boy Dave would shrug. "Still a bit cold, innit – for going out?"

"It was colder before, and you never minded. Anyway, you can come round ours."

"Why? What's happening?"

I normally gave up about then. And off I would go – on a really long walk back across the black tarmac of the schoolyard.

That weekend, me, Boy Dave and Ryan did manage to get together to play football on Saturday morning, but instead of meeting up in the afternoon like we normally do, Boy Dave said he'd promised to "just pop up to TC's" and Ryan said he had to go into the town to get some things for an urgent experiment "of vital importance".

It was the first Saturday afternoon I could remember when I hadn't had anyone to kick about with. I didn't want to hang round the house all day, so after lunch I took Nemesis for a walk along the river. I like Nemesis, but she's not the sort of dog that chases sticks or does normal doggy things, so you can't exactly play with her. Still, she snuffled along beside me in a friendly sort of way, sometimes running off into the woods and then joining me on the towpath a bit further on.

As for me, I tried to enjoy the walk. There was a fresh spring breeze, and the bluebells made a nice-looking low blue mist through the trees, but there was a grey sky overhead and everything felt wrong.

Even though I supposed I could go up to TC's any time and join in, it would have felt like surrender somehow.

I must have been daydreaming for a while because I suddenly realized that I'd walked a bit further than I'd meant to. Instead of trees on my left and houses on the opposite riverbank, there were fields on either side with some sheep grazing. I needed to get Nemesis back, because she isn't very good with them.

I looked round, peering through the long grass and nettles beside the path, but Nemesis was nowhere to be seen. I turned back to scan the trees, but she wasn't dashing out of the woods to find me either. At least the sheep seemed calm, so she couldn't be with them.

I was just about to turn back and look for her when I saw a small dark flash disappearing into the old stone sheep hut a bit further up the path. She must have crept through the grass and rushed on ahead. I got the lead out of my pocket and held it behind my back; then, keeping my eyes on the sheep hut to make sure she didn't come out again, I jogged towards it.

It had been ages since I'd gone in that sheep hut. Older kids sometimes hang there, so we keep clear. When I bent down and stepped inside, it seemed really dark at first. I closed my eyes and blinked hard.

When I opened them again, I got the fright of my life.

There was someone else in there, sitting with his back against the wall. His legs were straight out in front of him and his head was tipped back. The person was youngish; maybe eighteen, nineteen, with trainers and a hoodie like me. As my eyes adjusted to the gloom, he started to look familiar. Then I realized: it was Chiggley, Craig's old mate, who had tried to nick the pool money in the Black Horse the other night. I looked around. The sheep hut was full of old fag ends and beer cans, and covered in graffiti. It seemed like a weird sort of place for Chiggley to have settled down for a nap.

Nemesis, who had been bowling around, was now standing next to Chiggley, looking down at him with a serious expression on her furry brown face. Then she licked his hand. He kind of stirred but didn't wake up. For a minute I stood looking down at him, not quite sure what to do. It's funny looking at someone when they're sleeping; you can see all the details of their face and they don't care. Chiggley's mouth was a bit open and his skin looked pale and sort of dry. In the dimness his eyes were just circles of shadow.

Whenever I'd looked at him before, it had been secretly and I'd been trying to seem cool like him. I wasn't thinking that now, though. It just felt strange and a bit wrong. What if he was only pretending to be asleep and was just waiting for me to go? He'd think I was weird staring at him like this. And even though he'd been nice to me when I was a little kid, he had stolen all that pool money the other night. Maybe he'd changed over the years and become really nasty. Or maybe he'd think I was judging him and being a little creep sticking my nose into his business because of what had happened.

Well, he'd have got that wrong. I figured I had enough to be worrying about without older kids conking out in uncomfortable places. The whole place stank as well. Then again, some of them seemed to like things stinky and dirty. Take the hut at the skate park; they'd made that disgusting. Give me Boy Dave's nice clean garage any day.

I clipped Nemesis back on to her lead and started back along the towpath. Boy Dave's dad had done the garage out especially for him. It was great, with a little fridge for our fizzy orange, and beanbags to sit on, and . . . ARRGH! I suddenly felt really angry at myself for thinking about it all again. Feeling angry didn't do any good, though. It still didn't stop the horrible homesick feeling for how things used to be.

Sighing loudly, I decided that this was one of the most difficult problems I'd ever tried to sort out. And the one person, in the twelve years I'd been on this planet, who had always been there to help with whatever problems came along, was the person causing this great big one in the first place.

The way I saw it, if I wanted to have Boy Dave as my friend, I didn't have any choice except to go along with playing the games. I'd never understood before why on telly one kid doesn't really want to do something – like drugs or smoking or crime – but they go along with it anyway because their mates are doing it. Now I realized that being lonely and feeling left out could be a really good reason.

I sloshed along the towpath, where on my left, the muddy river was rushing in with the tide, getting higher and higher all the time, and a thought started to bug me. What would I do if I had to choose between following Ryan and Boy Dave into something I really didn't want to do or never hanging out with them again? I'd never seen it that way before. After all, most of the time we'd always agreed on things anyway. Up until TC, that was.

I thought about this as the trees of the wood rustled and the shadows between them became longer and darker. And Nemesis, who kept trying to pull away down the riverbank, got dirtier and dirtier. I realized that I hardly ever spent time on my own. You notice things a lot more when there's no one else with you – like the way someone must have cut all the dead branches down and put them into piles. I thought that me, Boy Dave and Ryan could make a bivvy one day, and then, straightaway, had a horrible unfamiliar thought that they might not want to.

Maybe it was the shadows and the idea that it would soon be dusk – or maybe it was the cold wind starting in off Crow's Ridge – but something made me think back to Chiggley in the sheep's hut. You're not meant to interfere with older kids, and definitely not meant to tell grown-ups their stuff. But what if he was sick or something? What if he'd had too much beer to drink? There'd been enough cans scattered about on the floor in there. Older kids sometimes do some really weird stuff, but there had definitely been something not right about him just sleeping in the cold like that.

I slowly got out my mobile phone.

For a second I thought of Boy Dave, but he would probably be right in the middle of a game, and anyway why should *I* be the one to call *him*? I stared at the display a while and then slowly punched in another number.

"Hullo!" My dad's gruff voice sounded in my ear.

When I'd finished telling him about Chiggley there was a long pause; then Dad said, "All right son, leave it with me. You get yourself off home."

I was almost at the bridge and back into the village

when I noticed two big, burly figures coming towards me. I jumped as a giant hand came down on my shoulder.

"All right, son, only me."

It was my dad. He was with PC White.

It's not often that PC White and me are actually pleased to see each other, but he said, "Well done, Jordan, you did the right thing. The paramedics have taken the young man out across the field. They're on their way to hospital now. I've rung Mr and Mrs Chiggley and let them know what's happened. Mr Chiggley asked me to say they're very grateful to you."

"Why?" I stared. "What was wrong with him?"

Dad put his arm around me and took Nemesis' lead. "Kid's had a drug problem for a long time. Seems he might've overdosed. It's lucky you found him when you did. Come on." He put his arm across my shoulders. "Let's get you home."

PC White went off in the direction of the sheep hut and me and Dad carried on in the other direction. After a bit, Dad asked, "What are you doing out on your own, anyway? Where's the Boy?"

I shook my head. I didn't want to talk about it. Instead I asked, "What about your work? I thought you said you had to work today."

"It's not important," said Dad quickly. "I wanted to see you home safe."

I blinked. It seemed strange having my dad "see me home safe".

For a bit we walked on in silence; then Dad said, "Promise me something, Jordan?" I nodded. "That kid back there in the sheep hut – promise me that is never going to be you."

I didn't answer at once. I thought about my dad and how grumpy and bad-tempered he was and how cross he always got with me. And, for some weird reason, how brilliant his arm felt around my shoulders. I watched his big, long shadow bumping along the ground next to mine. And I thought about what he'd asked for longer than I normally think about anything.

Then I said, "I promise."

That Monday it was weird to see Boy Dave waiting at the end of Hangman's Lane for me as usual.

"All right?"

I nodded. "You?"

"Yeah."

That was it. We walked up to school together as usual and that evening me, Boy Dave, Ryan, Daisy and Claire made a huge bivvy out of the sawn-off tree trunks.

Making bivouacs is normally a lot more fun than anything you can do with them afterwards. When it was finished I think the only person who really wanted to sit in it was Nemesis. The rest of us sat outside by the river, bobbing our torches off the water and picking out the face on the moon. It was fuzzy with cloud and just starting to wane. The nights would get darker now until it was just a tiny sharp curve above the hills.

I'd already told Boy Dave and Ryan about Chiggley in the sheep hut, but Claire and Daisy wanted to hear all about it too. When I'd finished,

Claire said it was sad, but Daisy said it was his own fault.

"Do you know if he was all right?" asked Claire.

"Well. . ." I shrugged, trying to sound cool about it all. "Dad's going to ring PC White and find out."

"Text me when you get any news."

"OK." I bobbed my torch over hers on the surface of the water. "Gotcha!"

But when I got home, no one had heard anything. Still, Mum gave me a hug and said, "See you have got some sensible bones in your body after all."

And Dulcie looked as if it was a lot of fuss about nothing and said that in the old days some very respectable people used to take laudanum for quite minor ailments, but in those days people knew how to conduct themselves and just became a little wild-eyed from time to time. And Joanna asked if everyone thought she should have her hair done on the morning of the carnival or whether it would be better to have it done the day before and just sleep sitting up. Best of all, though, Dad gave me a tenner.

By the next day, I had almost decided that all my worries about Boy Dave were over. We had art as the first lesson, which, by way of unusual surprise (not), was all about the Easter Parade.

Our old art teacher left before Christmas. Mum said this was something to do with stress, although

I don't really see how doing the crossword while everyone draws a cheese plant is stressful. Anyway, at our school now the teachers all take it in turns. One week we might do a drawing of the cheese plant, then next time, maybe a pot made out of clay sausages, or a sea picture with lentils. Our art room is like a museum of ancient relics of half-made crumbling pots and paintings because we never have time to finish anything. I wouldn't mind, but they'd managed to keep the Easter Parade thing going for weeks. Not only that, but the lesson was being taken by the least artistic person in the whole school.

Mr Jefferson used to be in the army, but unfortunately he doesn't realize that he has now left the army and is a PE and maths teacher, and that we are only kids, not recruits who must be tortured. He also has no sense of humour at all but can run very fast, which makes it important not to let him catch you doing something you shouldn't be doing. Anyway, Jefferson had obviously decided not to bother with art and was going to do what he called "logistics" instead.

He made us stand in a line with our hands behind our backs while he explained the "logistics" of the Easter Parade.

"This 'ere is the convoy." He tapped some oblong shapes on the whiteboard with his stick. "What will be setting off at ten thirty hundred hours precisely. Order of vehicles will be as follows:

"Number One vehicle: DeMontfort syndicate with flower-petal vehicle with designated 'uman flowers personnel kitted out in Easter bonnets what are too big.

"Number Two vehicle: bearing mascot large model rabbit what is not a true likeness (As it turned out, this was going to be very true).

"Number Three vehicle: His Majesty King Henry's syndicate what is 'uman" (he peered at his notes) "baby chickens and others similar. To the right and left flank of the aforesaid vehicle will be 'uman rabbit personnel what will distribute eggs from baskets.

"Number Four vehicle: carnival dignities what will wave to the crowd.

"Number Five vehicle: Thomas Payne syndicate with goats because they would not lend us lambs. Also on board will be 'orrible cardboard daffodil item.

"Number Six vehicle: Mr Fern's year ten break-dancing crew what is a load of girly nonsense and is not in keeping with the spirit of the day."

Jefferson (who obviously wasn't enjoying carrying out these particular orders) had gone a bit red and sweaty-looking, but he carried on bravely. "To the fore and to the rear will be marching bands playing well-recognized tunes what sound rubbish because they is not solid marching music specially written for trumpet, fife and drum. Ahh, yes." Jefferson stopped, looking disgusted, and his expression became wistful as he beat out a little rhythm on the whiteboard. "The diss'nant tones of fearless trumpet. The relentless heartbeat of the army drum. The upliftin' melody that puts mettle in the hearts of men."

Boy Dave muttered, "The neighing of the horses."

"The flying of the arrows," I muttered back.

"The clash of sword on armour."

"The noble exploding of the cannon."

The clumpy squeak of Jefferson's boots on the floor "what" we should have heard a bit earlier, and the next thing we knew, he was staring down at us from glinty eyes.

"You is giggling," he told us, "like girls."

He frowned and looked round, as if confused. "And I wonder what it is – that is making you giggle? Perhaps an amusing little joke that you wishes to share with us? An anecdote from some 'appy occasion that tickled your sense of 'umour? Perhaps," he suggested pleasantly, "the vicar did something untoward at your auntie's tea party?"

By now the whole class was cringing and me and Boy Dave were trying to mentally shut down all the nerve pathways to our ears before they were blasted to bits.

"Step out," invited Jefferson, "and tell us what it is

so we all may . . . *giggle*."

Embarrassed, we shuffled out in front of the class. I took a deep breath. "Er. . ."

Jefferson shoved his face so close to mine that our noses touched.

"I . . . DIDN'T . . . LAUGH," he yelled. He swung round and glared evilly at the rest of our class. "Did anyone else LAUGH?"

"No," they said, cringing pathetically.

"NO!" yelled Jefferson in my face again. "NO ONE ELSE . . . LAUGHED."

He took a big lungful of air, and I was just imagining life as a deaf person, when the door opened and the headmistress come in.

"Ahh, Mr Jefferson, it's you today. Good. Just what we need, a firm and steady hand!"

Jefferson stood proudly to attention. "Ma'am!"

"Bunting, Mr Jefferson," she told him, "we need large amounts of bunting. These would do." She pointed at a pile of half-finished paintings. "Waste not, want not. Perhaps some members of your class could transform them into gaily-painted triangles on a string. We need about a hundred metres."

Jefferson suddenly looked peaceful and happy. His eyes swivelled round and stopped when they got to us.

The bunting making didn't go very well. Jefferson had provided us with a template to "ensure all is of a uniform standard" but if we had done it how he wanted we would have been there for weeks. Cutting the triangles out took ages and there wasn't time for the paint to dry so we had to stick the paper over the string while it was still wet. Also the colours got mixed up. So although the bunting started off as gaily-coloured triangles, it soon became a line of squishy, brownish lumps of quite varied shapes.

It's strange how something can be so irritating and, at the same time, so boring that your brain cells start charging into your skull just to put an end to it. By the time we'd finished, we would be like crazed old men with long white beards who had been captured by evil blood-drinking people, and who had been kept in an underground cave with the skulls of past prisoners. Everything we used to know would be like a distant dream and we would clutch at each other's faces and go, "Yes . . . yes . . . I do remember. . . It was the bunti . . . i . . . iiiii." But then we'd forget again and go back to mumbling.

Ryan, who had been assigned to giant rabbit duties, wandered over. I think we were hoping that he'd thought of an idea for doing the bunting more quickly, but he had other things on his mind.

"I've been making a few suggestions about the rabbit," he said crossly, "and my offer of expertise and advice has been met with ignorance and suspicion."

"We could use some expertise and advice," I said hopefully.

"At the moment," continued Ryan, ignoring me, "it is to be a giant brown Easter bunny that has a movable paw."

"You mean like mechanical?" asked Boy Dave (Ryan loves mechanical things).

"No," said Ryan disgustedly. "Not mechanical; on a *pivot*." He seemed to have taken it as a personal insult. "With strings on either side, which are to be operated *manually* so that it can wave."

"Tut," we said. "Fools! Now help us with the bunting."

Ryan sighed and peered at our "workstation".

"It would have been easier to paint the sheets of

paper before you cut them up, possibly using a dip system. Secondly, rather than trying to cut out diamond shapes individually, you'd find it easier to fold the paper into squares and cut several at a time."

Me and Boy Dave thought for a moment. We had to admit he was probably right.

"I think," said Boy Dave, "that if we'd started off like that it would probably have been better, but it might be a bit difficult to get it going now."

We looked at the huge mess. Even Ryan had to agree that it was probably too late.

As soon as the bell went for break, Boy Dave disappeared off somewhere. I thought he'd just gone to the toilet and I stood watching Mr Fern's break-dancing crew. They had pushed some school tables together in the schoolyard so they could pretend it was the back of a truck. Mr Fern, who has spiky dyed blond hair and an earring (even though he's most likely at least forty, which is pretty sad), sweated madly and tried to get down there with the brothers.

"Matty, cut in now with the handsprings. Can you go right over? Oh . . . oh well . . . it'll come. Attitude on the back row, please."

The "crew" did finger shapes and jiggled, and took it in turns to shuffle round like someone had nailed their heads to the floor. Cal Mockford's brother did actually manage to get his feet off the ground and go up on his shoulders but then stayed there waving his legs like a beetle, with his face bright purple, until Fern said, "Oh . . . oh well" again. "That one needs a little work, Kev." And yanked one of his legs to get him down.

Joanna and Collette and some of the other girls from their class stood round going, "Woo, yeah," and one of the "crew", who obviously found this really encouraging, did almost manage a head spin, but then fell off the table and had to go to the office. Collette's brother, Jamie, wasn't so daring. He stayed with the slow somersaults, and just as you thought he'd stopped, off he would go again, round and round, while Fern and the others went "YO" in an encouraging way and looked embarrassedly at the ground.

After a bit it seemed like a shame for Boy Dave to be missing it all, so I set off to look for him. After wandering about for a while I found him sitting on a bench playing Nintendo DS with TC.

"Come and have a look at the break-dancing," I told them. "It's like old people on ice."

Boy Dave looked up. "Oh," he said. "Yeah, whatever."

He was eating one of TC's cereal bars. They'd obviously done a couple of packets already. There were wrappers everywhere.

TC said, "I don't really enjoy break-dancing."

"That's not the point, they're . . . oh, forget it!"

As I turned to glance back at them slumped over the game, it was like looking at a pair of lifeless, blobby twins.

That was when I finally decided to ask Ryan for help. Up until then, I hadn't liked to admit how much it was bugging me, but he'd probably guessed anyway, and Ryan's brilliant at problem-solving. That Monday I tracked him down to one of the computers in the school library. He was looking at what I took to be the surface of a mouldy-looking planet.

"It's actually a cheese," he explained.

"Oo-kay. And what's it for – this cheese?"

"I suppose . . ." Ryan squinted and peered more closely at the mouldy blue lumps that filled the screen, ". . . somebody's going to eat it at some point."

"Yuck."

"Not really. I shouldn't think it's different from any other sort of cheese of that kind."

"Except that now it's a celebrity cheese, probably with many deranged fans," I pointed out. "Not mentioning anyone in particular. Why are you looking at it, by the way?"

"Well, its maker put it on a web cam so we can watch it mature. It's quite interesting, actually."

I think that was when my confidence hit an all-time low. My best mate liked playing computer games more than hanging out with me, and my second-best mate preferred watching cheese mature.

"Em. . ." I said, turning away, completely crushed, "when you've finished, I wanted to ask your advice."

"Oh. Right. You should have said." (Ryan loves being asked for advice.)

He shut down the cheese and swivelled round in his chair. "To the problem in hand."

"Well." I wondered where to begin. "It's about Boy Dave."

"Yes, I've been wondering about that."

I was surprised.

"What were you wondering?" I asked cautiously.

"Well, he's changed quite a lot in the last month. For a start, he's gained something in the region of at least a stone and a half and doesn't go out much any more. I thought it was quite interesting, actually – the timescale, I mean. I would have expected such physical and emotional changes to take longer, which led me to wonder if certain sorts of technology could serve to bypass normal habit-forming patterns. By which I mean embedded habits are generally notoriously difficult to alter, but. . ."

"Yes," I said hurriedly, "but we need to keep this so

as I actually know what you're saying. How can we stop it getting worse?"

"Hmm." Ryan put his chin in his hand. "A sort of reversal, you mean? I suppose it would be something similar to a chemical substitute – in so much as it would fool the brain into believing that one substance was actually another, but this time without addictive properties."

"I don't think he's got that sort of problem," I said hastily. "It's more that he's got like TC and doesn't see the point of reality any more."

"It's exactly the same sort of thing," explained Ryan. "It's just that it would be about trying to replicate the fantasy world with something similar, but real, and gradually introduce more and more reality until he got used to it again."

With its usual bad timing, the bell went for lessons then, and we made our way slowly back across the yard. It was good to have Ryan helping, but I didn't really see how what he'd said would solve anything. As far as I could understand it, we were going to have to find a way of becoming gangsters or parachuting into battle or something before Boy Dave would even consider getting involved in real life again. None of it seemed very likely – in our village, if you even bang off a rookie (which is what the farmer uses to scare crows, so personally I can't see how they mind us doing it), they call an emergency meeting of the village hall committee and you end up being grounded for weeks.

"I'll tell you what," said Ryan after a bit. "Come up to my mum's studio after tea tonight. I should have a solution by then."

Ryan's great like that; he thinks everything's possible and it's just a case of finding out the right way to do it.

We met in Ryan's mum's barn a bit after seven that evening. She uses it as an art studio and her latest things were pinned up all over the walls. They looked as if they'd been painted on the insides of old stuck-together cereal packets.

I stopped in front of one that looked like a burned fried egg with two shocked-looking yolks for eyes.

"This one actually looks a bit like a face."

"Yes," said Ryan gloomily. "It's one of her environmentally friendly portraits. It's meant to be Mrs White. They were going to do a sort of *Calendar Girls* thing at the Women's Institute but with just the heads. My mum was meant to be doing them all as portraits but it didn't go very well. She said she was just painting them as she saw them, but they turned violent and threw a jam jar at her."

"It's better than Mrs White's actual head," I pointed out.

"That's the sort of thing my mum said."

"Was that when they threw the jam jar?"

"No; that was when she tried to incinerate them with her sculpture-welding stuff. I've had a think about our problem," Ryan said, changing the subject and looking suddenly more cheery. "And I've reached the conclusion that it's doable."

I sat down on the floor, unscrewed the cap on a fizzy orange and rolled another over to him.

"I think," said Ryan, "the trick would be to get them somewhere under false pretences."

"Them? You mean TC as well?"

"Well, if TC comes, Boy Dave will have nothing to do, so he'll have to come too."

"Don't you think TC's a bit too far gone?"

"Probably. But we only need to get him off the games long enough to cure Boy Dave."

Ryan did his pointy serious look. "The first thing will be to find a distraction which works. We'll create a real game, but it will be like a computer game. Then we'll get them to play it. You know – a bit like how we got TC to go on the golf buggies."

I tried to feel good about this, but when it came to putting things into action, it was starting to sound a bit like my dad's pool tips.

"I suppose we could do a war thing in the woods," I suggested.

"Not unusual enough. Boy Dave will think the woods are too familiar and boring. If this is going to work, we need to create a whole virtual landscape with lots of challenges, so they keep on wanting to come back."

There was silence while we both stared at Ryan's mum's environmentally friendly face things. Probably this is the moment where I should have fixed my gaze on one and then gone, "Brilliant! The egg! That gives me an idea." But obviously this never happened. So far as I know, there's no such thing as a terrified-food computer game, and I wasn't about to be the sad loser who invented one.

It helped a bit that Claire and Daisy chose that moment to come round.

"We got bored," explained Daisy, "so we thought we'd come and help with your problem."

"Ryan says that Boy Dave just sits and eats and plays computer games and never sees the light of day any more," Claire said to me.

"He told you?" I spluttered through a mouthful of fizzy orange.

"Well, we're your friends, aren't we?" said Claire sternly. "I think it's really nice of you to try and stop him before it's too late. I heard about one boy who got so bad he wouldn't even get up from the games to go to the toilet. He had to go in plastic bottles."

We all went "Eeyuk" and I stopped feeling cross. After all, right at that moment, I could do with all the friends I'd got.

We carried on trying to think of real but computery-type games.

"How about a spaceship sort of thing?" I suggested.

"Or a fantasy one with dragons," said Daisy.

"What about a ghost one about the Lavatories?" asked Claire. "We could dress up in black hats."

"I think," I said hastily, "ever since the sauna thing. . ."

"Well, how about another house then, like one that no one lives in. We could do it up like a film set almost?"

And that was my genius idea moment. Up until then I'd been thinking we'd have to make the whole thing ourselves, but *now*. . .

"I know," I said excitedly, "just *exactly* the right place!"

That night before tea I went into the kitchen, where Mum was spooning gunky homemade stew on to plates.

"I was wondering when Dad was taking me to see how the new community centre was going," I asked casually.

There was a longish pause.

"Oh well." I shrugged. "It doesn't matter. I wasn't really that interested anyway."

"Did Dad say he was going to take you, then?" asked Mum.

"It's just. . ." I tried to look as if I was hiding my disappointment. "He was saying about how you have to . . . er . . . put the concrete in before the . . . er . . . lighting and that. Don't worry, I must have got it wrong."

Mum gave me one of those forgetting-all-the-bad-stuff kindly looks they give you when you're ill.

"I've noticed that you and your dad are getting on well at the moment, Jordan. You know it means a lot to him, don't you?"

I think this was actually an invented thing. Mum is a bit like Joanna in that way and sometimes confuses TV-type feelings with real ones.

"Yeah," I said thoughtfully, "I suppose we have been getting on a bit better. Anyway, don't bother reminding him about my trip to the community centre. He's probably really busy."

When Mum reminded Dad for me, because "I'd been too shy to ask", Dad gave me a really suspicious look, but she'd done the sick-child face, so not taking me would have been the same as him refusing to call the doctor when I was ill in bed, saying, "Mother, why is the light so dim?"

My trip to the community centre after school that Thursday meant listening to a lot of very boring explaining, and having to lay a brick in front of Dad's mates, but I managed to find out everything I wanted to know:

- The community centre wasn't going to be used for at least another three weeks
- Generators are really, really loud
- And (especially good) my dad and Big Dave would be contracting out most of the electrical and plumbing jobs and wouldn't be around much.

"It's perfect," I told the others. "Now all we need to do is work out the game."

Over the weekend we planned it really carefully. There would be three teams: the Bladers (on rollerblades), the Wind Riders (on bikes) and the Surfers (on skateboards). Players had to reach certain destinations, like the stepladder or the fire door, and stop the others getting there first. Ryan wanted to make up a complicated points system, but me, Claire and Daisy thought it would be best to just see who took the worst hammering. We would attack using chest blasters (flour) and blood-head finish (water bombs), and make feather traps with feathers from pillows, which could be released by pulling a string on the ceiling. This was a bird-head assault and needed careful cunning and planning.

We figured the details of exactly how to win could be sorted out a bit later, once we'd tried the game out a few times. There was still no electricity and it would be really dark so we would wear straps across our chests with torches fixed to them. The Wind Riders would have headlights as well. We called the game Death Chase Olympia (DCO), but then Claire said it should have an X in it, so it became DXO instead.

That Monday at school, TC and Boy Dave were sitting on the bench as usual when me and Ryan went up to them.

"Hi," said Boy Dave, looking bored to see us.

Ryan got straight to the point.

"Do you still do virtual games," he asked, "or is it all just sitting down now?"

"We do some virtual," TC told him, "but lately we've been playing a lot online."

Ryan said casually, "We've been doing a lot of virtual stuff lately."

"Well, yeah, but. . ." I widened my eyes as if I was trying to shut Ryan up. "You know . . . we agreed not to say. . ."

TC looked interested. "Which one is it?"

"DXO," said Ryan, as if they should have heard of it.

"Seriously?" TC frowned. "What d'you play it on?"

I nudged Ryan and made as if to turn away. "Come on, we've got to plan the traps for tonight, remember?"

"What traps?" demanded TC.

Ryan looked at him like he was stupid. "Blood head, bird head. . ."

"Skid ride and chest blasters," I added. "Artillery freeze out." (We'd decided to have water guns as well.)

"What's the mission?" asked Boy Dave.

I shrugged. "All different ones. It's too complicated to explain. You'd have to see it, really."

TC and Boy Dave looked at each other.

"We-ell," said TC slowly, "we're kind of in the middle of a game with some kids in Japan right now."

But Boy Dave shot me a strange look.

"Is it round at yours, then?"

"Course not. We don't want anyone to know we've got it. I suppose we could take you to where we keep it – if you were really interested."

"Nah," said TC after a bit. "We'll get it on trial and check it out sometime."

But maybe Boy Dave was actually a bit jealous at the idea of his two old mates having fun without him, because he asked crossly, "Tell us where it is, then."

I could see him desperately trying to think where it could be.

"Can't tell you," said Ryan sharply. "Serious players only, I'm afraid."

Boy Dave stared in amazement and I felt a bit mean.

"Come on." Ryan turned and started to walk off. "We've wasted too much time already."

It took all my willpower, but I turned away as well.

Without another word, we started back across the schoolyard. There was an indignant yell from behind us, but we pretended not to hear. Seconds later we heard running footsteps, and Boy Dave grabbed me by the shoulder.

Me and Ryan had said we were having tea at each other's houses so we could make sure everything was set up exactly right. If the plan was going to succeed, everything had to go like clockwork.

We had arranged to meet Boy Dave and TC at seven that evening at the end of Hangman's Lane, but as we stood waiting for them, shivering in the dark, I knew we were thinking the same thing – would they bother coming at all?

It had been twenty minutes, and I had literally just opened my mouth to say we should probably forget it, when two tiny specks of torchlight came wobbling slowly towards us down the path.

"Phew," said Boy Dave when they finally got to us. He was really out of breath. "I'd forgotten how far it was."

"Well, it's only a little way now," we said encouragingly.

As Boy Dave and TC puffed and panted along behind us, Ryan whispered, "It would be easier if we had something to push them in."

"They need to retrain for proper actions, remember?" I whispered back.

"I know. But I'm seriously starting to doubt if they're going to make it."

He had a point; it was like watching two people walking through quick-drying cement. They'd brought some "snacks" for the journey and all the fumbling about and packet opening took up time as well. We'd be lucky to get there by daybreak.

Eventually, though, with the help of a whole box of cereal bars, cold pizza and four cans of Coke, TC and Boy Dave managed to keep themselves going until we got to the community centre. And, even if I say it myself, the labyrinth (as we were calling it) looked brilliant. Claire and Daisy, already in torch harnesses, were gliding up and down the corridor on roller boots, and in the darkness, they really did look like virtual shining characters.

Now came the difficult bit. Boy Dave and TC were already completely pooped and we somehow had to persuade them to play the game. Boy Dave, who had been peering through the entrance of the community centre, gave me a bit of an odd look.

"Do our dads know about this?"

I felt a sudden little prickle of irritation. Boy Dave would never have asked such a stupid question a few months ago. It was hard to think he'd changed so much.

"We would like to present to you DXO," I said grandly, not bothering to reply.

"You two are the Wind Riders," said Ryan. "You have certain powers and certain disadvantages. Firstly, you are the swiftest of all the players, but you must beware the slip paths and you may carry no shields. The ride is a perilous one, with many chances of death. Your weapons are these freeze guns. . ." He shoved two mega water blasters into their hands while hustling them towards two bikes propped up against the wall, as Claire and Daisy glided over and popped torch harnesses over their shoulders.

It was a brilliant atmosphere. You could only just see the outlines of the windows, dimly lit by the moon outside, and there were no doors, so the rooms along the corridors were eerie, dark, gaping holes. Everything had that stony smell of cement, which added to the feeling of being underground.

"You have the advantage of search beams," continued Ryan, pointing to the headlights on the bikes. "But these are only activated while you're moving. Stop and you lose the advantage. Once installed in your chariots, you may not leave them. I must also warn you that there are many traps set within the labyrinth and, as first-time players, you will have no knowledge of how to avoid them. You need to develop your skills in order to reach the next level. . ."

Ryan went on and on, explaining about when you could be paralysed and when you could use bird head or blood head and the bombs and so on. The weird thing was how seriously Boy Dave and TC were taking it.

"There is one more thing you must know," said Ryan as Boy Dave spun back the pedal on his bike. "If you are unfortunate enough to enter the room of death, the game is over."

"How will we know it's the room of death?" asked TC. His eyes were big in the torchlight.

"Because you will die," said Ryan.

The first few games had been mainly just attacking each other madly, but as time went by, we started to take it a lot more seriously. By the time it was mine and Boy Dave's turn to be Wind Riders, we were deadly determined to win.

We leaned forward, waiting at the top of the corridor, and it was so quiet we could hear each other breathing. Our right feet were on the pedals of our bikes and our left legs were ready to push off. Our eyes strained into the darkness, and it felt as if a monster might come flying out of there at any second.

Putty glows in the dark, and the new glass in the windows glowed in long white patches. They looked like the sort of blobby drawings you do as a kid. Along the corridor, the concrete twinkled with tiny silver specks in the faint moonlight.

It seemed like a long, long time before my mobile went. The jangling ringtone echoed over and over, away down the corridor. Quickly Boy Dave clicked a button on his, and far off in another part of the building I heard Claire's phone ring.

"Ten," said Ryan's serious voice at the other end of my phone.

"Ten," repeated Boy Dave into his.

"Nine," said Ryan.

"Nine," repeated Boy Dave.

"Eight."

"Seven."

"Six."

"Five."

"Four."

"Three."

"Two."

"One."

"ATTACK!"

Whooping and yelling, we were off, flying through the darkness. The headlights of the bikes jumped across the floor, flickering across the doorways and walls like an old silent movie. Catching the corner just in time, we slammed down our feet, and with trainers almost sparking on the floor, banked sharply. At the same moment a wall of lights came flying towards us. The Bladers (Claire and Daisy on rollerblades) were charging at what seemed like a hundred miles an hour and they were *screeeeaaaming*!

We didn't stand a chance. At the last minute, the lights parted, passing on either side of us, and stinging water bombs exploded on our faces. Laughter echoed away up the corridor.

"Right," yelled Boy Dave, "that's it!"

I wiped my face with my dripping sleeve and pedalled after him.

"They think we're going to try and go round this way and head them off when they come round the block," panted Boy Dave, "so they'll come across the middle instead." He veered sharp right, into the first corner of the X corridor. "Come on, there's a bird-head trap in the middle. We'll get them there."

By now we were pedalling right for the heart of the building. The two corridors that crossed in the centre were the longest and darkest. Not even moonlight made it through the windows there. Everyone must have decided to play by stealth tactics, because it was eerily quiet.

We had almost reached the middle where the corridors met, and there was still no sign of anyone. Slowing my bike, I pointed to the ceiling a few feet away. Just caught in the beam of our headlamps was the edge of a bulky lump above: one of the sheets filled to the brim with feathers. At that same moment, the lights of the Bladers appeared at the other end of the corridor. I reached out for the string to release the trap.

Suddenly, as if from nowhere, missiles came flying. It was too late to dodge or turn around. Me and Boy

Dave flailed helplessly as our mouths and noses filled with flour. Through the dust, I could just about make out another set of lights on either side of the cross. It was Ryan and TC. They must have been lying in wait for whoever tried to release the bird head first. Meanwhile, the Bladers were almost upon us.

With a huge effort of willpower, I forced myself to open my eyes and lunged for the string. They were almost certainly preparing for another volley of blood head or chest blaster, but I yanked down hard and a mass of feathers flumped from the ceiling on to their heads.

It was just the distraction Boy Dave needed. As the Bladers yelled and waved their arms, he aimed his freeze gun and fired. The Surfers, Ryan and TC, gasped and yelled as Boy Dave made two direct hits. Before they could recover, they took a few from me as well. Ryan, now defenceless, kicked his skateboard into action and flew off, back down his corridor to the nearest weapons station. Feebly TC tried to speed off after him, but skateboarding wasn't his strong point.

As he wobbled dangerously off towards the wall, me and Boy Dave mercilessly sped up after him, ready for a drive-by of flour bombs. Meanwhile, the temptation of lone prey proved too great, and Claire and Daisy flew off in search of Ryan.

TC, realizing his situation, jumped clear of the skateboard just before it hit a door frame. As we continued to bear down on him, he did just about the only thing he could do. He bolted into the room. Seconds later, there was a terrible shriek.

A bit more cautiously than we had been going to, we followed him in. TC was staring, frozen in terror, at the hideous, howling image of one of Ryan's mum's WI portraits. Even I'll admit it was horrific. The portrait, which was about as tall as me, was lit up by my dad's free-standing car torch so the dreadful, contorted, howling face was all you could see in the darkness.

After managing to avoid it for three games, TC had found the room of death.

He didn't seem to mind being pelted with the last of our flour after that. What with his not-very-useful grip on reality, I think he was quite glad to find out that he was still alive.

As it happens, TC wasn't the only one to be unnerved by the WI death beast that night. To get it down to the community centre, Ryan had ridden his bike with the picture strapped to his back, and quite a few cars had caught it in the headlights and wobbled a bit. Ryan explained that his mum had done it "after the style" of someone called Bacon – which might explain why Mrs White had looked like an egg.

Boy Dave grinned over at me and raised his hand in a high five. And at the exact moment our hands met, it was as if something really important clicked back into place. It should really have been Ryan's hand up there, though. This was the best plan he'd ever had. And even more than that, it had actually worked. With a massive feeling of triumph, I turned and bombed my bike as fast as I could through the darkness, yelling all the way.

After a few hours of playing, we were really hot and sticky, so we went to sit outside in the freezing night air.

It was a bit of a shock when we saw each other. With all the feathers and flour and stuff, it was like being surrounded by chicken people.

We had an argument about who had won; then Claire said, "I suppose we'd better clear up."

"We must make sure we remove all traces that we've ever been here," I agreed.

Boy Dave pulled a face. "Why?"

I gave him a look. "If our dads find it like this in the morning, we're dead."

"But they won't be here tomorrow," said Boy Dave. "Everything blew up at Barcombe and the electrics have to be fixed up there first. I know because I heard Dad working out all the money they're going to lose. It's going to take at least a week before the sparks can get down here, and no one can get on with anything else until they do. Dad's really grumpy about it."

Mine probably was too, but I'd been so busy with

setting up the labyrinth I hadn't been paying much attention to what was going on at home lately.

Ryan took a glug at the water bottle. "In that case, we may as well keep it as it is and just do a sort of giant spring clean at the end. After all," he nudged me, "we're probably going to be coming down here most nights."

The thought of leaving the labyrinth as it was made me feel a bit nervous, but I knew he was right. It's like putting things away in drawers and cupboards – there's normally no point, because sooner or later you're going to want them out again.

"OK," I agreed, "but when we're finished, it's got to be as if we were never even here, OK?"

"OK," said the others, nodding seriously.

The next thing to do was to plan the next night's traps.

"I could get the pillows off my mum and dad's bed," offered TC, "and their duvet. There's some stuff in the spare rooms as well."

"Probably just the ones from the spare rooms," we told him, "and maybe some power sticks, if you can get them."

"It might be a lot to carry," said Ryan. He was probably remembering how hard it had been for TC to get here just carrying himself. "We'll come and give you a hand."

"And. . ." I stopped, wondering how to explain.

"*Sometimes* grown-ups – like your mum and dad – don't *really* understand why you might want to use something for . . . er . . . something else."

"I could ask Isabelle," suggested TC, "and Davina's probably got a lot of feather things."

"We find," helped Boy Dave, "that it's best to never *tell* anyone in your house what you're doing – like, if you need to borrow something, just take it and put it back later when you're finished, as if you'd never even touched it in the first place."

"So," said TC slowly, "I borrow the pillows and duvets and power sticks, and when we're finished, I put them back as if I'd never touched them in the first place."

"Ye-es," we agreed.

"But not telling grown-ups or Davina is vital," said Ryan. "It will inevitably mean GAME OVER."

"Oh, right." TC's frown cleared. "So they're sort of the enemy?"

We gave a sigh of relief. There was hope for him yet.

When I got home I took off my chicken-boy clothes and hid them in the front garden. There was an awkward moment when Dad saw me rushing up the stairs, shivering and wearing only my pants.

But he just said, "What are you doing out of bed, Jordan?" and assumed I'd come in ages ago.

38

The next day was Tuesday, and me, Boy Dave and Ryan were walking across the schoolyard first thing when we saw TC. He was carrying a briefcase.

"It's the Easter Parade Cup," he told us. "I'm to give it straight to the headmistress."

"Let's see?"

TC looked doubtful. "It will have to be only a quick look. Dad drove me down this morning specially. He said I was to take it to her office straightaway."

It was smaller than the golf cup, but otherwise pretty much the same. On it was written *Hatton Down Easter Parade*.

"I think they put the winner's name and date on it afterwards," explained TC.

"Hmm," said Ryan. "It seems a bit of a waste, though, to just leave it hanging around in the head's office gathering dust for a whole week."

After school we all headed up to The Cedars. The plan was, we would wait round the back of the house under an archway on the path while TC got the feathery things. Then we would run down the side paths, lob the stuff over the wall at the end, and pick them up afterwards.

After what seemed like hours, TC appeared at the back door. He puffed out to where we were hiding and flumped down a couple of pillows.

"They're a lot heavier than they look," he said, wiping the sweat from his forehead. "I don't know if I can manage any more on my own."

"Well, I can't help." Ryan gave us a bit of a look. "If I get caught, they'll think I'm off to the pamper suite."

"I'll do it," I said hurriedly. Not that I particularly wanted to, but being too near the computers might not be very good for Boy Dave at this stage in his cure.

As usual, the house seemed deserted at first, and TC and I got the duvet from the spare room without any problems. We were just about to sneak down with it when there was a bit of a commotion in the living room below.

"IF YOU SAY AGAIN I MUST TIDY UP MY WRAPPERS I WILL DO A GREAT BIG POO POO ON YOUR HEAD!"

Davina (at least I supposed it was her and not TC's mum) made her point by blowing some extra-loud echoing raspberries.

Over the raspberries Isabelle's voice said crossly, "You make mess, you tidy!"

There was the sound of a scuffle, and footsteps thudded hurriedly up the stairs towards us.

"Quick," I said to TC, "your room."

Bundling TC and the duvet up the small flight of stairs, I shoved them both into TC's den. Down below in the house, the sound of running and yelling continued. Meanwhile TC's eyes had glazed over and he had switched on one of his computers.

"NO!" I hissed. He stared at me blankly. "We have things to do, remember?" Desperately I looked around the room. "Look, we could. . ." I rushed over to the window. Far down below I could see Boy Dave and Ryan huddled underneath the archway. "We'll throw out the duvet instead! That way we won't even need to carry it down."

"That window!" TC gave it a disgusted look. "Someone should paint it black. Then I wouldn't need curtains."

"No. The window is good." I shoved him over to the glass. "You see? Your friends are waiting. Down there in the daylight. They're counting on us." I had a sudden idea. "You have to help me get it open."

Sweeping away a graveyard of dusty, crusty dead flies, I scraped back the catch and shoved up with all my might. By the feel of it, the window hadn't been opened for years.

"Come on," I said impatiently to TC. "Help me."

Much to my surprise, TC's shoving made all the difference.

Almost as soon as he put his weight against the frame, the lower window shot open so fast that we almost fell out.

"Cor." I wiped the sweat from my eyes with my hand. "You're a lot stronger than you look."

TC looked pleased and went a bit pink.

"I suppose I do quite a lot of wrestling."

"No – I mean really you are – in real life. C'mon, help me get this duvet out."

I signalled madly to the others waiting under the archway, and then me and TC shoved the duvet through the window. With a final push, it fanned out like a large white jellyfish and headed towards the ground. Ryan, finally sussing out what we were doing, pelted across the grass from the archway just in time for it to land on his head. Without even bothering to throw it off, he ran back across the grass to the path and flitted through the archways, down to the bottom of the garden.

"Brilliant." I dusted my hands together. "Now, even if we are caught, it'll just look like we were just hanging out."

Cautiously I poked my head out of TC's door.

**39**

"I tell you," TC's mum's voice floated up from the landing, "it was not an intruder. I saw it FLY past the window. Then when I ran to look it GLIDED away down to the bottom of the garden."

"But, Bosie, hon. . ." This was Tom.

"I knew we should never have moved into such an old house," she interrupted him. "There must have been so many tragedies here in the past. I did get the feeling, you know, that it was trying to communicate with me. Maybe it was trying to tell me something that could put its poor tormented soul to rest. I think it was trying to lead me down to the bottom of the garden to show me where. . ."

"Hon," said Tom again, "you've been watching too much *Most Haunted* again."

"And you know, I only saw one apparition, but I *sensed* there were more. Now I come to think of it, I'm sure there were two spirits present; one who was just trying to tell me something –

that was the poor lost soul I saw – and then another more malevolent one. You know, I'm almost certain it was her. . ." she dropped her voice "*murderer*!"

"Honey," said Tom, sounding a bit bored, "if it makes you feel better, we'll call in that woman, but if you ask me it's a waste of money."

Luckily, they had started off down the stairs again and, not so luckily, seemed to be heading for the kitchen. Still, that meant there was at least a chance of sneaking out through the front door.

Cautiously we tiptoed down the rest of the stairs, swiped (what turned out to be) some really heavy golf clubs from Tom's office and, dragging them behind us, sneaked out through the front. When we met the others, Boy Dave sounded pretty relieved to see us.

"You were gone ages. Tom's been out here wandering around. What happened?"

"Hmm," said Ryan when I'd finished. "It's a shame we didn't think of doing it as a haunting in the first place. Still, with any luck they'll think they've got a poltergeist." (In the end I should think TC's mum and dad thought they had quite a lot of things, but I'll come to that.)

Right then, so far as I was concerned, everything was going great. Spring was here and it wasn't turning out so bad after all. And before too long we'd have the brilliant long, hot (well, hot-ish) days of summer. I always think every summer is the best one I've ever had, but this one. . . I just knew this one really would be.

The game that night was brilliant. The mission was to get the sacred chalice (Easter Parade Cup) from the room of death and carry it on top of your power stick to the other side of the labyrinth. You had to get right to the top of the stepladder with it, which meant you'd won. It's a bit difficult to describe exactly what happened in the game – basically each team started as far away as possible from the room of death, then we rang through to each other, did the countdown, and after that we could do anything we wanted to get there, grab the chalice and run for it. Meanwhile your opponents had to try and knock the sacred chalice off your stick with theirs.

No one actually managed to get up the stepladder that night, but as TC said, it normally takes a bit of time to get up all the levels.

We were cooling off afterwards and planning the next night's game when Ryan coughed.

"Er. . . I think the time has come to share with you my most complex and effective invention to date."

"Is it something for the labyrinth?" asked Boy Dave.

"It wasn't built for that purpose," said Ryan, "but we can use it, yes."

After that the most we could get out of him was that it was going to need a few of us to move it and that all would be revealed the next night.

Dad normally leaves for work about the time I get up, so the next morning I was surprised to see him still chomping toast at the table.

"You're off late today."

"Yer, well." He pushed the toast rack at me, but not before he'd grabbed another two bits and left me the burnt one. "Me and Dave are off to see a bloke about a housing development."

As usual for mornings, Dulcie was doing her crossword. This means she can pretend to be concentrating and ignore everyone or join in when she feels like it. She must have been in the mood for an argument because she said, "We don't need any more nasty little orange houses!"

"I'll tell you what," said Dad (who can never resist a brick argument). "Why don't you write to all the stonemasons and tell them you don't like the colour orange. Then you can moan about whatever other colour houses instead." He was trying to be sarcastic, which never works.

"Those nasty little bricks aren't the only building

material," said Dulcie snobbily. "There's sandstone and slate and, as the Prince of Wales rightly points out, we should recycle our lovely old buildings instead of knocking them down."

Dad hates the royal family. He slopped his cup down crossly and stood up.

"Too expensive. And when the Prince of Wales actually knows anything about death-trap old buildings, he can rebuild them himself."

He was just about to stomp into the hall and get his boots on when his mobile rang. A few minutes later I heard him talking.

"Was it a fox, d'you think? . . . Chickens? Nah, mate, there's nothing like that round there. Vagrants, maybe? . . . It's not going to get in the way of the job, is it? . . . Righto . . . righto . . . will do."

He came back carrying his boots and absent-mindedly started putting them on in the living room, which he's not allowed to do.

"Er . . . what was that about chickens?" I asked.

Dad tutted. "Sparks have just rung from the community centre. Something's got in and made a right mess of the place. They thought maybe a fox had dragged a few chickens in there, but I can't see where they'd have come from."

I stared. This was great! If they were going to blame all the feathers stuff on foxes, we'd *never* have to clear it up.

"That's most likely it," I agreed, trying to hide a big grin. "Probably a whole pack of foxes and . . . hens." I tutted and said what people round here always say about foxes. "Vermin!"

"I don't see how it could be." Dad shook his head. "There's no coops anywhere near."

"They're most likely wild chickens," I told him knowingly, "that make their nests out of dead leaves and that."

"My money's on vagrants." Dad didn't seem to have heard. "At least the doors are going on today; that ought to put them off."

From brilliant to disaster in two seconds.

"Ye-es," I said slowly. "That probably would put them off a bit."


I suppose I was waiting for the right time to mention the doors, but I didn't really get a chance. Being honest, I think I was trying to kid myself it wasn't going to happen; then, by the time evening came, we had other things to think about. It was time to see Ryan's invention.

Claire and Daisy had rugby practice so it was just me, TC and Boy Dave who headed down to Ryan's after school.

"I've had to borrow my mum's barn," he explained. "There wasn't enough room in the laboratory." By which he meant his shed with black singed bits all over the roof. He was making his way towards an enormous eight-foot-tall lump, covered by a dust sheet at the far end. When he got there he waited until we were all standing round expectantly, before pulling the sheet away with a dramatic swoosh.

"Behold!" he said grandly. "My Mark 1 mechanical deluxe Easter rabbit.'"

We goggled.

"Easter *rabbit*?" I asked after a bit.

There were quite a few ways you could describe Ryan's rabbit, but rabbit wasn't really one of them. It was a bit like the sort of snowman you build when you've got bored of rolling the snowball round and round and end up shovelling piles of snow on instead. Except that those sorts of snowmen normally end up being quite small, whereas Ryan's rabbit was huge and made of some sort of cement-looking stuff. Also, it had obviously been built on a strictly "need to have" basis, in so much as it had a huge shocked-looking, gaping mouth (but no eyes or nose), and an enormous human-looking arm right in the middle of its body. I suppose its ears were rabbity-ish, but they were thinner and more horn-like than a normal rabbit's, and not really in the right place.

"The very same!" said Ryan triumphantly.

"Er. . ." I said hurriedly. "It's amazing. What's it made of?"

"I had to use an artistic method, which is something

I normally try to avoid." Ryan pushed his glasses knowledgeably up his nose. "However, the casing which houses the mechanism is made of a chicken-wire frame, with strips of material dipped in plaster. These are then wrapped around the frame to give the rabbit the shape that you now see before you."

At least that explained why it looked like a mummy.

"As you know," continued Ryan, "I was displeased with the way the school Easter rabbit was designed, and detected many flaws in both its construction and lack of well-conceived mechanism. I therefore set out to make my own rabbit of similar proportions, but with greatly improved functioning due to a superior design and an internal mechanism. As opposed to," he added disgustedly, "a *string* which you *pull*."

"It . . . er," I nodded at the arm, "waves, then?"

"Not only that. . ."

Ryan disappeared round the back of the rabbit, and a few seconds later a loud clunking noise started to come from its stomach.

"Observe!" he said dramatically. Then, a bit more normally, "Actually, you might want to get out of the way a bit."

Slowly, like a giant upside-down pendulum, the rabbit started to wave. Gently at first, but as it gathered speed its enormous paw began to lurch wildly from side to side. *Clunk-clunk, clunk-clunk* went its stomach, speeding up in time as the arm-arc made 180 degrees. We watched, mesmerized, and might have gone into a trance except that suddenly, without warning, a rugby ball-shaped missile catapulted out of the rabbit's mouth, hurtled across the room, and lodged itself in an old settee.

"Wow," said TC admiringly. "Now do it with a sticky grenade."

Ryan, who was standing on a chair, poked his head round.

"Impressive, isn't it?"

"What *was* that?" asked Boy Dave, staring at the settee.

"An Easter egg," said Ryan grandly. "While the float is going along, the rabbit will wave, and, at the same time, it will fire Easter eggs out into the crowd."

Secretly I didn't think the school would agree to swap their brown, string-operated rabbity-looking rabbit with Ryan's mechanical mummy one, but he was so proud of it, I thought I'd better not say so.

"It's great," I told him, "but I don't see how it could actually be moved."

"Oh, it's not as hard as it looks. The only really heavy bit is the arm pivot, but I can take that off. After all, for the purposes of the game, we're not going to need it to wave, just fire missiles. I can simply replace the pivot mechanism back into the body in time for the Easter Parade. All we really have to do is to get underneath it and walk."

It took a bit of experimenting, but it was quite easy to crawl underneath. The head was still quite heavy, but at least once Ryan had taken the arm off, we could look through the hole and see where we were going.

I can't pretend the trip down to the community centre was a whole lot of laughs. Nettles were springing up on either side of the path through the woods, making it narrower, and there was a woman walking her dog who screamed. By the time we got there, me and Boy Dave were feeling a bit grumpy and were just starting to enjoy breathing in air which wasn't full of plaster of Paris when Ryan said, "This door never used to be here."

Oh NO! I felt myself go red. In all the rabbit excitement, I still hadn't mentioned what Dad had said about the doors. Luckily, before I had to decide whether or not to own up, Ryan reached out and tried the handle.

"Rule number one of science," he told us in a superior way, "never assume that something is so until you've proved it to be the case."

There was a click, and the door swung open.

"Wow." I stared. "My dad's going to be mad. They were meant to be keeping out foxes and vagrants."

Too late, I realized that everyone was looking at me.

"Oh. . ." I spluttered nervously. "Yes, of course, that's us. Er . . . guess what? I've got some good news."

I explained about the conversation that morning, but left out the knowing about the doors bit.

Boy Dave peered down the darkness of the corridor. "We might still have a problem. I think there's someone here."

A small square of light was falling out into the hallway further up.

"I'll sneak up and have a look," I said bravely.

"No, wait. Leave it." Boy Dave shook his head. "If it's one of Dad's blokes, he might recognize you. We'll just sneak in and open a window or something. With any luck, by the time we get back from tea, they'll be gone. We can get the bombs ready at home and set the traps when we get back."

Ryan sneaked through and opened the fire exit; then we hid the rabbit (or RPG, as we were calling him) behind some trees and headed off home for tea.

Boy Dave had been right. When we got back, the building was in darkness. It was a bit of a problem getting the RPG through the fire exit, and we ended up having to just wedge him in front of it at the end of the corridor, but in a way that worked quite well, because it blocked off one of the other corridors and made the game harder.

Ryan showed us how to fire him by climbing up the stepladder, pulling really hard on a lever until a little drawer came out, putting the bomb into it and letting go. We were going to use him for water bombs, but because they were smaller than Easter eggs, they slithered around in his mouth and ended up going off in all directions. The advantage was that you could do several at once.

We began with me and TC on the skateboards. TC's skateboarding had improved a bit, but it still wasn't up to much. On the other hand, I'd thought up a really good plan to make up for it. TC could pretend to have the sacred chalice on top of a power stick; then, when Boy Dave and Ryan gave chase, we could draw them into a bird-head trap. We'd done this loads of times, but this time I'd switched off all my torches. I was really pleased with this, because no one had thought of it yet. I hid in the darkness and chuckled to myself – they wouldn't even see me coming!

As planned, a few minutes later TC, pretending to have the sacred chalice on his power stick, paddled along the corridor, followed by Boy Dave and Ryan on the bikes. They were catching up fast but the corner slowed them down a bit, which gave us just enough time. Quickly I opened the door and TC paddled past me into the room. My hand was on the string of the bird head and Boy Dave and Ryan were almost within range when TC, minus the skateboard, backed out again slowly.

It was obvious something was wrong. TC had stopped dead, and was staring as if in a kind of trance. Boy Dave and Ryan skidded their bikes to a halt.

"What?" I asked crossly, really miffed that my trick had been ruined.

In the torchlight, TC's eyes were like saucers.

"I've found the room of the dead," he said hoarsely. "Dead people. All laid out. Rows and rows of them, dead. In the room of the dead," he added in a whisper.

Remembering what he'd been like with the WI death beast, I tutted crossly and poked my head round the door.

It was the scariest thing I've ever seen. They really were there: rows and rows of bodies laid out neatly in lines. And all around, in between the rows, were burning candles. I stared, not able to believe my eyes, and Boy Dave and Ryan crowded in behind me.

"Oh wow," said Ryan after a while in a low voice. "It's obviously a religious sect that have come in here and committed mass suicide while we were having tea."

"Oh my GOD!" Boy Dave's voice right beside my ear made me jump. "One of them's still alive."

But even as he spoke, there were faint stirrings all across the room. Some of the dead people had started to try to roll over and get up. We should have run away then, but we were fixed to the ground with terror. Horrified, we watched as one of them got to its feet and came tottering feebly towards us.

"Quick," yelled Ryan, "BIRD HEAD!"

Hearts thumping, we swung ourselves to the sides of the door frame. As the zombie emerged from the room, Boy Dave pulled the string. There was a flurry of feathers and a hideous screech as the creature was engulfed. But now there were more of them. Crawling and muttering they came, reaching for us with outstretched arms and clawing hands.

"I'll man the rabbit," yelled Ryan as he raced for the RPG.

TC, who seemed to have recovered from his shock, decided to take charge.

"Quick." He grabbed Ryan's bike. "You stop them escaping and I'll get them back on their stations."

But there were hundreds of them now, charging through the door and out into the corridor. Desperately we pelted them with flour bombs, while Ryan rained down volley after volley of water bombs.

"What about TC?" yelled Boy Dave. "We can't just leave him!"

With a final burst of flour he ran into the room. Without thinking, I raced after him.

TC was spinning and skidding wildly, swinging his power stick above his head as he tried to herd the zombies back to their places. Outside in the corridor, some of them must have tried to escape through the fire exit but found the RPG blocking the way, because there was a sudden hideous shrieking and a huge wave of them surged back down past the open door.

"BACK," yelled TC, obviously remembering Whipstaff. "BACK, AWAY."

I don't know exactly why it was – maybe it was because one of the creatures had looked a bit like TC's mum – but round about then I started to get a bad feeling.

"HIM!" yelled TC, before I could say anything. "He's the one who controls them!"

We hadn't noticed before, but at the front of the room was a man quietly sitting cross-legged on the floor.

"Woah," he said as TC charged towards him, "take it easy."

At that moment Ryan burst in. "It's all right. I think they've gone!"

"Hello," said the cross-legged character. "I'm Jason."

My bad feeling got worse. By now I was hoping that we really had unleashed a killer zombie sect on the village.

"Why were all those dead people and candles here?" I asked, not sure that I wanted to know the answer.

"Yoga," said Jason calmly. "I was teaching a class before you came in. What are you doing here?"

"We . . . em. . ." said Boy Dave slowly. "We were just checking that everything was all right. We heard some noises and we knew the place was meant to be closed, so we thought we'd better check that everything was OK. We thought all those people were dead."

"Well, it is called corpse pose," said Jason, considering. "We give in to gravity and still our minds. It's meant to be a form of complete relaxation."

By now, me and Boy Dave were already imagining our own corpses when our dads found out.

"But the community centre's not open yet," said Boy Dave desperately. "You had no right breaking in here and holding a secret yoga class."

"Well, we were meant to be up at the village hall, but the ceiling sprang a leak, so we were allowed to start here a few weeks early."

There was silence while we watched the last slivers of hope disappear.

"I suppose," Ryan pushed a feathery set of glasses up his nose, "they'll all complain now."

"I expect so." Jason smiled peacefully. "In a long line . . . like the tail of a snake. Well," he added, "I suppose that's what a snake is, really – just one big long tail. I mean, when you contemplate it, there isn't much more to a snake."

We goggled.

"Don't you . . . em. . ." I stopped and tried again. "You don't seem to be as cross as grown-ups normally get."

Jason shrugged and lay down flat on his back.

"We learn to accept. That way, at least we can see." He sighed in a relaxed sort of way. "We might not be able to do anything about it, but at least we can see. Anyway, I think the energy in the room is better now they're gone."

For a second I wondered how easy it would be to make our dads do, like, a really quick crash course in yoga, but this was seriously clutching at straws. Still, it was something to think about in future. It would be great if, every time something bad happened, our dads just lay down on the floor and said, "We learn to accept." Then again, the way things were going, I wasn't too sure I wanted to think about the future right at that moment.

On the way home, though, we started to cheer up a bit. After all, Jason hadn't asked who we were, and it had been pretty dark. Probably all anyone had seen was headlights and torches. And when we were playing the game, we couldn't even recognize ourselves behind them. With any luck, they'd just put it all down to the vagrants.

Ryan had been really upset because we'd had to hide the RPG in the woods, but we'd promised to go and get him at the first opportunity, and the most important thing had been to get out before PC White arrived.

It was gone ten by the time I nervously tried to sneak up the stairs at home, and it was actually a relief when Mum shouted from the living room, "I said nine!"

If she'd found about the yoga people, she would have been saying a whole lot more. I tried to carry on up the stairs.

"Jordan! In here now."

I was obviously going to get a lecture about *where have you been? What have you been doing? If your dad and I say . . . then that's what we mean (and blah blah).* Still, under the circumstances, even that was pretty good going.

I went into the living room slowly, trying to look really guilty about being late back. Mum and Dad were watching TV and Dulcie was doing the crossword, with Nemesis snoring on her lap.

"Sorry about that," I said. "I forgot the time and then my phone didn't seem to be able to get any signal, otherwise I'd have rung. Anyway, I'd better get straight up now – school tomorrow and all that."

I was going to try and sneak off but something about the way they were all staring at me made me stop.

"Sorry, was there something else?" I asked politely.

"What have you been doing?" asked Dad in an odd sort of voice.

Mum was a bit more direct, "*Jordan!* What's all that stuff down you? Where are all those feathers from?"

I looked down at my sweatshirt; it was white with

dried flour and water, and fluffy with hundreds of feathers stuck into it like cement. This was terrible! What with all the fuss, I had accidentally gone home dressed as chicken-boy.

Desperately I tried to think of an excuse and remembered what had happened to Dad once, when he'd been driving the van.

"Yeah, I know." I tutted and shook my head as if I couldn't believe it myself. "There I was, just running along, and a bird flew right out in front of me."

There was a bit of a pause; then Dulcie said, "I daresay it was an early fledgling."

But the forces of darkness were gathering apace. I was halfway up the stairs again when there was a sudden great roar from the living room. And at the same time there came a loud knock on the door.

I met Boy Dave at the end of Hangman's Lane as usual the next morning. He was looking gloomy.

"I suppose PC White came round yours as well."

I nodded depressedly. "I still don't see how any of them could have recognized us."

"They didn't have to. You know how prejudiced they all are. They think everything is down to us."

"It's not going to be easy to get the rabbit back either," I said. "Now that we're grounded."

"I don't want to make it worse," said Boy Dave, "but I think there's a problem with the sacred chalice as well."

It was Thursday and we'd agreed the cup should go back today, because if we left it until Friday Miss Stormberry might get worried and phone Tom.

When we got to school, we made our way to a bench in a quiet part of the schoolyard and Boy Dave got the cup out of his school bag. Problem wasn't the word.

"It's mullered!" I stared at it in horror. "When did the handles go like that?"

"I know," said Boy Dave miserably, "and look at all these dents and scratches. I mean, all we ever did was ride it around on top of a golf club."

"Oh wow." I'd just tried to put the cup down on the bench. "It doesn't even stand up any more."

"We can't give it to her looking like that," said Ryan in a practical voice when we showed it to the others.

"I could say that's just the way it's always been," suggested TC.

We sighed.

"You've never really been in trouble with grown-ups before, have you, TC?" said Boy Dave sadly (by the sound of it, as usual, me and Boy Dave were the only ones who'd been blamed for the night before).

"I'm not normally much trouble," agreed TC. "Most of the time I just play computer games."

"Well," I said hastily, "it's good that you're learning a bit more about real life, but there is something you really have to learn right now."

"Which is," continued Boy Dave, "that we must NOT give the sacr . . . er . . . parade cup to the headmistress looking like that."

"What you have to do," I explained slowly, "is go and tell her that your dad is going to give you the cup to bring in on Friday, OK? You got that? Tomorrow."

TC looked confused. "But it won't be any different tomorrow to what it is today."

"Well, maybe it will and maybe it won't," I told him irritably, "but the thing about getting into trouble is you always, *always* try and put it off until the last minute. After all, you never know: there might be a huge earthquake. The headmistress might die in the night. A meteorite. . ."

"We could assassinate her," interrupted TC helpfully. "Or maybe do an insurance fraud and throw ourselves under a car holding the cup and get lots of money and. . ."

Boy Dave sighed. "Look – right now we need to do stuff that won't get us into any worse trouble, OK?"

"Listen," said Ryan seriously. "Can you remember what you have to say when you go to the head's office?"

"MY DAD IS GOING TO GIVE ME THE CUP TO BRING ON FRIDAY," TC said in a mechanical robot sort of voice.

"Er. . ." Boy Dave looked pained. "Is there any way you could make it a bit more natural-sounding?"

"That was natural-sounding," said TC. "MY DAD IS GOING TO GIVE ME THE CUP TO BRING ON FRIDAY."

In the end we quit while we were ahead. At least he knew the words, and with any luck the head would just think he was a bit strange (and, let's face it, she wouldn't be far off the mark).

After TC had gone, we sat round looking gloomily at what was left of the Easter Parade Cup.

"I'll just have to try and weld it back into shape," said Ryan eventually. "That's all we can do."

"Have you got a welder?" I asked.

"My mum does. Last weekend she welded an old digger on to a line of dustbins." He sighed. "Apparently it's called 'Crocodile'. Anyway," he brightened up again, "it definitely works."

Later that night (after Mum and Dad had moaned on and on [again] about trusting me and how could we and what were we playing at and la la, etc. And Joanna had sweetly suggested that I should, like, maybe go to a special clinic where celebrities go when they've totally messed up their lives) Ryan sent us a text. It said: *cup melted*.

Weirdly enough, just as we thought we were so completely, totally doomed, we were saved by a stroke of genius. And you'll never guess whose it was. That (deadly Friday) morning we were kicking round in the schoolyard contemplating a life without money or freedom when TC came and found us.

"I've got another one," he announced proudly, plonking a brown suitcase down on our laps. "The Whipstaff character thinks some things have gone missing from the safe up at the club so he asked my dad to keep it until the day of the tournament."

Trying to feel more hopeful than we really were, we watched as Boy Dave clicked the latches.

"But this is the golf club cup," he said tiredly when he saw it. "It says *Chalk Hill Golf Championship*."

"My dad was keeping it in his safe," said TC, looking pleased with himself, "but I took the key and got it out again. Then I locked the safe and put the key back in his desk in the right place, just as if I'd never taken it in the first place."

Even though the situation didn't seem to have got much better, I couldn't help feeling a bit proud.

"It's a good idea in a way," I told him kindly, "but if we give the headmistress this cup, then your dad will have nothing to give the golf club, and she will wonder why it's got golf stuff written all over it."

But already the cogs of Ryan's brilliant and twisted mind were churning.

"When exactly is the golf club tournament?" he asked thoughtfully. "Morning or afternoon?"

"Afternoon," said TC. "The medium is coming in the morning to try and exorcise all the spirits that haunt our house. Quite a few of them got into my mum at yoga as well and she accidentally brought them home, so now we have some that weren't even there in the first place."

It seemed best to leave that one where it was.

"Hmm," said Ryan hurriedly, "and the parade is in the morning." He looked at it thoughtfully. "So theoretically *this* cup could do both jobs."

"Except that someone will win it in the morning and take it with them," I pointed out.

"But what if that person was us?" said Ryan. "Then all we'd have to do would be to get it back to Tom in time for the golf championships."

"We haven't got a hope of winning it, though," I pointed out. "Me and Boy Dave don't even know what house we're in."

"That's not a problem," said Ryan. "Ours can be an independent entry. We'll just explain that we're nothing to do with the school. In the meantime, if we can cover up the golf-type writing, we've bought ourselves another day to get our float sorted out."

That morning after assembly we all had to go to the gym, where the whole rest of the school were madly rushing round getting the floats ready for morning.

Jefferson had put little notices up at different parts of the hall saying number one convoy, number two convoy, etc., and was stomping round with a clipboard and a stick yelling at everyone.

We scuttled crab-style over to where some year sevens were smearing the carnival thrones with gunky silver and gold paint from some little tubes.

"Mind if I borrow that a minute?" I asked, swiping the tube from the sticky grip of a year seven.

He glanced nervously over at Jefferson, but before he'd plucked up the courage to say anything, we were already sitting in a circle on the floor of the school showers, with the cup, like a heart transplant patient, in the middle.

Ryan, surgeon-like, squeezed a splodge of glue from a yellow container across the golf writing.

"This stuff sets like rubber," he explained as he smeared a layer of silver over the top. "Ri-ight. Now. If I just wipe the excess stuff away. . ."

He rubbed over the writing a couple of times with his sleeve, then held the cup up to the light.

A huge sigh of relief echoed round the shower room. It had worked! If you really, really peered at the cup, you could make out where the engraving had been, but the writing was such small thin lines anyway, the glue had filled them in almost perfectly.

"Right," said Ryan to TC. "It should be dry by break. You can take it to the head's office then. Meanwhile we'll just have to hope she doesn't ring your dad."

"What did she say?" asked Boy Dave nervously as TC came out of the head's door, looking pleased with himself.

"She said," TC frowned, "THANK YOU VERY MUCH, DEAR. I'M SURE SOMEONE WILL BE VERY PLEASED AND PROUD TO WIN IT TOMORROW."

"Now all we've got to do," I said, "is make sure that's us."

At last we were all starting to see a light at the end of the tunnel.

"The school floats are rubbish," said Boy Dave. "We can definitely do better than that."

"And our Easter rabbit is far superior," agreed Ryan.

There was a bit of a silence.

"You think he should . . . er . . . actually be *on* the float?" I asked nervously.

"Certainly. We'll get the Easter eggs that are meant to be handed out to the crowd, and use him to distribute them instead. It'll be a real eye-catcher."

"We-ell," said Boy Dave, "in that case, he's going to need a bit of work on his appearance. At the moment he's too hard and lumpy and his ears are like horns."

"And he has a not-very-rabbity giant arm in the middle of his body and no eyes or fur," I pointed out.

"*Fur* isn't a problem!" said Ryan irritably, as if we were just nit-picking. "We can cover him in *fur*. And I'm sure it'll be easy enough to give him some temporary eyes. As for the issue of his mechanical arm, this is irrelevant. A rabbit's arms are not an important part of his anatomy. Ears, yes – they are a distinguishing feature for a rabbit, but mine has very prominent ears."

"Well, whatever," I said hastily. "He needs a bit of work. And we only have until tomorrow to get a truck and enough brilliant Eastery stuff on the back of it to win the cup."

"I can get us a truck," said TC. "I'll just tell one of the drivers that my dad said we must have it for our own special float. We can use my Carnival King one."

We stared at him with new admiration. All we needed to do now was find some great stuff to put on it, enter the parade, win the cup and whiz it back up to Tom's safe before the golf tournament.

"One thing, though," said Ryan thoughtfully. "What if your dad tries to get the cup out of the safe in the morning and it isn't there?"

"That's all right," said Boy Dave. "TC can take it up to the golf club later and say he was just giving it a polish. Tom'll go, 'That's my boy, with his kind heart' and everything will be fine. We all know that in his eyes, TC can't do anything wrong."

TC looked suddenly thoughtful.

"I don't think I know when I'm doing things right and when I'm doing them wrong," he said. "I would probably find it easier if there was a sort of score card, like a carnage count or something."

"Take it from me," said Boy Dave seriously, "when you start knowing the carnage count, your problems *really* begin."

I felt nervous that evening as I sat down to tea. The plans for tomorrow were basically the sort that would be really good if they worked and seriously bad news if they didn't. I definitely wasn't in the mood for any more lectures from Mum and Dad. Luckily (in a repulsive sort of way) Joanna was in full Carnivile Queen mode.

"I'll be on my throne," she was telling Mum, Dad and Dulcie, although Mum was the only one trying to look at all interested. "And at my feet will be my attendants, kneeling. Collette is going to be in, like, green and brown netting to represent all of nature, and Danielle has, like, a brown dress with green netting to represent Mother Earth and all that she gives us – like a kind of a harvest theme?"

"Or spring?" suggested Mum.

"Just everything growing, and I'm like the sunshine that makes it all possible. There'll be yellow and white flowers laced through my hair and I'll have some in a bouquet as well, to throw to small children. You have prepared my gown, haven't you?"

"Yes, of course we have, love," said Mum. "It's all laid out on your bed."

Joanna put her hand on her chest and sighed massively.

"Thank goodness. I had a really bad dream last night that I came to get ready and my dress wasn't there! I know it was only a nightmare but it was so real. I think it's all the pressure I've been under these last few days. Auntie Dulcie, have you finished the gold sequins?"

"Sequins, dear?" said Dulcie, looking a bit vague.

"Yes, Auntie," said Joanna, going a bit pink, "the three lines of sequins that cross over my bodice!"

Dulcie hunched over her plate and carefully carved a carrot into small chunks. "I . . . hmm . . . that's strange, I don't rem. . ."

Mum glared at her. "Yes, darling, Auntie Dulcie *has* finished the sequins on your bodice. And on the shoes."

Joanna breathed another massive sigh of relief.

"It's just so stressful. It would be the worst thing if I came to find the dress and there was something wrong, just like in my dream. I mean, it's hard enough with the other girls being so envious. Collette and Danielle haven't actually said anything but I know they're really miffed at having to wear earth colours. I mean, I have tried to explain that nature *is* basically brown and green. And it's not as if they can wear anything really bright because then my outfit won't stand out. And in my role as Carnival Queen I have to represent, like, sunshine and hope for the future and the bursting out of new flowers and. . ." Joanna's brain cell almost burst out itself at the effort. "The rebirth of Christ," she finished.

Mum said, "Well, we can't wait to see you in the procession tomorrow. Can we, Dominic?"

"No," said Dad gloomily.

My nervous feeling was getting worse by the minute. With all the worry of making plans, I hadn't even thought about the terrible possibility of Mum and Dad being there. I looked over at Joanna, who was carrying on about how hard it was representing the whole of Easter. Talk about stress – if all I had to worry about was my dress not being right tomorrow, I'd be feeling great right now. As it was, an intergalactic space fleet battle had started in my stomach. Any minute now I was going to start clunking like the RPG.

By the time I woke up on Saturday morning I was feeling better, and at least we had the Easter parade as an excuse to go out because all the Hatton Down kids were meant to be up at the school. The plan was to get TC's Carnival King truck down to the community centre as early as possible and fetch the rabbit. Then came the tricky bit: raid Davina's bedroom. As Ryan had pointed out, "Davina's stuff is a whole lot better than anything we could have made ourselves. I mean there's a horse for a spring animal, flower stuff, and some great Carnival Queen things. Compared with our float, all the others will look like they haven't made any effort at all."

To begin with, me and Boy Dave had our doubts.

"But Davina's stuff is hideous," I pointed out.

"And really pink," said Boy Dave.

"And what if Davina catches us?" I asked as a sudden terrible image popped into my head. "She tried to poke your eyes out just for sitting on her throne. I hate to think what she'd be like if she found out we'd taken her whole bedroom and bunged it on the back of a truck."

"Whatever it is," said Boy Dave gloomily, "it'll involve an awful lot of 'poo'."

"I don't think that'll be a problem," said TC. He blinked as if he was just waking up. "Whenever we have the exorcist in, me and Davina have to go out. I expect my mum will make Isabelle take her somewhere in case she gets possessed by evil spirits."

It was hard to imagine an evil spirit being worse than Davina on her own; still, it was a relief to know she wouldn't be there.

"That's all right then." Ryan rubbed his hands together. "And as for all the other stuff, just remember that Easter Parade things are always hideous. And they are *always* flowery, queeny, pink and purple." He looked sternly round. "The only way we're going to win this is if we out-flower, out-queen and out-pink the opposition."

Me and Boy Dave knew defeat when we saw it. One thing was for sure – if we tried to do the sort of thing we liked, we didn't stand a chance.

Even though we had thought we were really early, a quick glance through the school gates showed the whole thing was depressingly well under way.

"Phew," said Boy Dave to the stocky shape of TC, who was loitering in the shadows. "You're here."

"Can you see your truck?" I asked him.

TC pointed through the gates. "It's the one with the purple flowers."

"Right," said Ryan briskly, "let's go and get it." To me and Boy Dave he said, "If they've got any other good stuff, we want it, OK?"

The schoolyard was in chaos and no one noticed as me and Boy Dave sneaked along the side of the first truck. Only the goats on the deck made the pupils of their eyes into little thin lines and gave us an evil look, of the sort that only goats can do.

On the other side from us Rhajni Singh was asking Jefferson nervously, "Are you sure they won't bite?"

Next to her, Steven Longacre dabbed his eyes feebly with a tissue and whined, "I think farm animals are one of my allergies."

Jefferson gave him a look that was almost as evil as the goats'.

"When you 'as 'ad to give your name, rank and number in a tent full of CS gas with no respirator," he told him, "that is when you knows the meaning of watery eyes. And when you 'as 'ad to recite a little poem" (he looked into the distance as if it was conjuring up fond memories) "still with no respirator, you do know the meaning of a runny nose. But what you 'as got is nothing what can't be sorted out with your little 'anky. Billy goats is vicious," he admitted to Rhajni Singh, who had gone red and started to sniff, "but these is tethered, friendly goats what is used to children."

The goats did the line thing with their eyes and chewed thoughtfully on the daffodil montage, while Rhajni and Steven climbed nervously aboard.

The next float was the Carnivile Queen herself. Joanna thought she'd been rebirthed and gone to heaven herself. She was sitting on her throne wearing her crown, with a flower carpet being arranged at her feet.

"If you see, like, a little child in the crowd?" she was telling two peeved-looking attendants. "You must throw them one of my flowers? And I'll smile and wave?"

Collette, who is normally Joanna's best friend, said, "Like, Joanna?" She gave the other attendant a look. "You is not the real queen."

Collette and Joanna hardly ever fall out, so it would have been great to stay and listen, but there wasn't time. And anyway the next truck was looking very promising. On the deck was the rival Easter bunny surrounded by his zigzagged papier mâchè eggs, some petal hats and, most importantly, four large baskets of real Easter eggs. Emma and Poppy were having their faces painted with black noses and whiskers and their bunny costumes were on coat hangers at the side of the truck.

It was one of those profiterole moments.

We hid amongst the trees outside the school gates and waited nervously. This was crunch time. Unless TC managed to persuade his dad's driver to do what we asked, we had no chance.

It was with a huge sense of relief that we heard the deep rumble of an engine approaching. Seconds later a lorry trundled through the main gates and hissed noisily to a halt. A bad-tempered, pale-looking man jumped down from the cab.

"This is Stanislaw," explained TC, poking his head out of the window. "He's Polish."

Stanislaw took off his baseball hat and stared.

"This people?" he asked TC.

"Yes," said TC. "They're going on the back."

Stanislaw huffed and puffed as if he'd been asked to shift a few elephants before shrugging as if the whole world was mad anyway.

"There is regulation against, but what can I do? I Polish worker. I get all bad jobs." He pointed to a small metal ladder up the side of the truck. "You go up here. Not fall off and break neck – this bad news for me."

It was great on the deck, like a huge wooden stage. As the lorry headed down the hill to the community centre I sat in the middle on TC's throne, framed by lumpy brown bunting, and started to feel really excited. We would be like gladiators in shiny chest plates returning triumphant from battle through streets of cheering crowds – victorious champions with our big shiny cup snatched bravely from the jaws of defeat.

Apart from a bit of green mould, the rabbit didn't look too bad for a few days in the wood, but Stanislaw wasn't impressed.

"Your father say you must have this *fing*?" he said to TC in amazement.

"Yes," said TC firmly, "you have to put it on the back. Then we must go up to my house."

Shaking his head, Stanislaw plonked his baseball cap back on, and with a bit of help from us, hoisted the rabbit on to the truck.

"We must be very careful," Ryan told him. "The head houses a delicate firing mechanism which is constructed to precision. . ."

But Stanislaw was already stomping back to his cab.

Once we got to The Cedars, me and TC tiptoed quietly in through the front door. If anything, though, the house seemed even more deserted than usual.

"They ought to be here," said TC, frowning. "I know it was today the medium was coming."

"Maybe it went really well and they've finished and gone out?" I said.

"Or maybe it went really badly," suggested TC.

We were in the hallway and were just about to give the all-clear to the others when we heard a strange noise. TC stopped and looked down at his feet.

"Umnlumnin ooooarrha mlmnmnm," chanted the floor. It gave a sudden muffled wail.

I clutched at TC's arm.

"Oh," said TC, perfectly calm. "Yes, I should have thought."

He showed me a door in the wall just outside the kitchen.

"The exorcists sometimes go down to the basement in case the spirits try to hide down there instead of leaving." (Just when you thought TC's family couldn't get any weirder).

"How many exorcists have your family had, exactly?" I asked politely.

"It's my mum's sixth sense. Spirits are always trying to contact her," explained TC. "Sometimes it takes a few goes to get rid of them all. Anyway, I hope it's them down there."

Gently I pushed open the basement door. At the bottom of a long flight of steps was a dimly lit room with what looked like lots of wine racks. The chanting had stopped and a voice was saying, "There's a lot of activity now. The spirits are telling us that they don't want me here. We must prepare ourselves for their anger."

I had a sudden flashback to a mouthful of cream and chocolate. It was the flowing lady with the fish lips from the party. Bosie's voice said nervously, "And what exactly do you think they might do?"

"They will try to frighten us into leaving by any means they can. We must be strong."

Tom's voice said, "I think I'll have another glass of Bordeaux."

Quietly I clicked the door shut again and headed out to give the others the go-ahead.

"It's all right," I told TC. "They think we're angry spirits."

It was like one of those house makeovers where a whole team goes in and clears the room. Up and down stairs we whizzed, with cupcake-shaped cushions, furry blankets, life-sized pony (with stable), bits of four-poster bed and other Carnival Queen-type stuff. Meanwhile everyone in the basement was obviously being really strong and the chanting kept up bravely. There was a dodgy moment when the horse kept going off, but I think the exorcist put all the carrot chomping and neighing down to evil spirits because there were quite a few muffled cries of "BE GONE!"

Back on the driveway, Stanislaw, looking totally miserable, loaded everything on to the truck.

"I'm not dressing up," said Boy Dave firmly, as we threw the last string of flower lights on to the back. "It's bad enough having a pink float without us dressing up as well."

"You'll have to," Ryan told him, "or you'll look odd in the queen environment. I mean, obviously I'll be the actual queen, but you'll have to be something."

"If we don't hurry up," I said sternly, "no one's going to be anything. They'll find out about the cup and we'll be in even more trouble than we are already."

"And that's saying something," said Boy Dave gloomily.

We were all set to go, but Stanislaw refused to budge. He had given up loading and was sitting down having his sandwiches.

"You come when I eat my breakfast," he told us (in the same way you'd tell someone they'd just run over your cat). "Now I must eat lunch too early and be hungry later."

The only way we could get him to move was by TC making him another packed lunch of cereal bars, Peperami sticks, crisps, cherryade, and a microwave burger.

We had decided the best thing to do would be to drive back to the school and park nearby. When it looked like the school parade were about to go, we would set off ahead of them. That way we would be the first float the judges would see, and because we would be up ahead, none of the teachers would get a good look at us.

We were busy arranging the queen things when TC – who had been lying on the four-poster bed eating an Easter egg and not really being very helpful – sat up suddenly.

"I've been thinking," he said.

We stared.

"Go on," I said cautiously.

"Well, we want to win the parade cup back, right? And we have to compete against all the other floats – like they're sort of multi-players."

"Yes, that's it," said Boy Dave impatiently. "But we'd better get on now." This wasn't the time to be explaining things game-wise. However, TC, who seemed unusually determined, ploughed on.

"Well, it seems to me that the best thing to do is just to make it *not* a multi-player game. It's much easier to compete against your own score than a load of kids in Japan who score really high. I mean, normally I would, but it just seems to me . . . well, anyway, that's what I thought."

There was a bit of an embarrassed silence, and then Ryan's eyes started to glimmer and he peered at TC interestedly.

"How would we do that?"

"Well, the *strategy* is that I would do the same with the rest of the trucks as what we did with Stanislaw."

Me and Boy Dave were struggling somewhat, but Ryan and TC seemed to have reached some sort of understanding. Ryan tipped his head to one side.

"How would you do that?"

TC shrugged.

"I'd say there'd been a change of plan."

It wasn't until after we arrived back at the school gates that me and Boy Dave understood any of this. From what we could understand, TC was just going to get us a load more truck drivers, but as far as we were concerned, Stanislaw on his own was bad enough.

It was coming up for ten, and if Jefferson's "logistics" were anything to go by, the procession would be moving off soon. I looked around our "float" and my heart beat faster with a mixture of nerves and excitement. Even me and Boy Dave had to admit it looked pretty good. The judges would be really impressed with our efforts. They'd probably think the pony was a real spring animal, and the bed and throne were way better than Joanna's pathetic queen things, especially with the cupcake and heart cushions all around.

Even the rabbit, who now had the eyes off Davina's poo bear, was wrapped in purple and pink furry blankets, with matching cushion covers over his ears, and looked a bit more like an actual animal. With any luck, once he was firing Easter eggs, no one would really notice his appearance anyway. I sighed with relief – we were finally on our way to Easter Parade Cup glory.

I should say at this point that this was a really, really stupid thing to do. Sighs of relief nearly always echo deafeningly across the universe, and the forces of disaster fly towards them like demons.

As soon as we pulled up outside the school, Stanislaw jumped down from his cab and marched meaningfully towards the school gate.

"Oi," yelled Boy Dave. "Stan! Where are you going? We need you."

Our relief and excitement morphed into a sort of

green jelly of dread as we stared after him. Stanislaw had obviously smelled a rat. He was going to dob us in. We were tiny seconds away from being in more trouble than – well – almost more trouble than we'd almost ever been in our lives.

"I go to swap," said Stanislaw without turning round. "I not like this job."

Phew. He was only going to swap (and once again the sigh echoed across the universe, etc.). Only this time it wasn't just us the disaster demons were headed for. Whenever I look back on this bit I always feel a bit sorry for Stanislaw and his pathetic attempt to escape.

A few minutes later an old boy in a flat cap appeared.

"Hello," he said. "The Polish geezer reckons you're doing 'is 'ead in, so I've come to take over. I'm Bert, by the way."

Then instead of getting into the cab, he settled down with his back to a tree and started to read his paper.

"Oh for goodness' sake!" said Boy Dave hysterically to TC. He sounded like one of our mums when they're tidying the house for visitors. "Don't any of your dad's drivers just get in and drive the lorries?"

TC shrugged. "I'm not sure."

But there was no time to discuss it. A sudden low

rumbling growl from the direction of the school froze everyone in their tracks. It got louder and louder as one by one the trucks started up their engines.

"Oh no!" I flapped frantically at Bert. "It's the school floats. They're coming now. Quick, we have to go."

Bert turned the page in his paper.

Ryan stood up imperiously from his throne.

"Driver," he ordered. "We must leave immediately! TC!" He gripped him by the shoulder. "It's time. Good luck."

And much to our surprise, TC bolted for the steps. As he threw himself down them, a soft voice said, *"Welcome to a magical fairyland, where all your wishes really can come true."*

Crouching behind the four-poster bed with the Easter eggs, we watched as TC ran out into the road waving his arms. With an urgent hissing of brakes, the first truck ground to a halt, and a horrified face stared down from the cab.

"Stan!" yelled TC. "Great, it's you. There's been a change of plan."

Back in the cab, Stanislaw made the sign of the cross.

"What does he think he's playing at?" demanded Boy Dave. "Tell him to get back here now before he draws attention to us."

But Ryan shook his head. "He's diverting the other trucks. It's what he meant by multi-players. The less competition we have, the better. Hopefully, by the time anyone realizes the school floats have missed the parade, we'll have won the cup and it'll be safely back at the golf club."

By now the rest of the trucks were swerving around ours and trundling off down the hill. As we risked a peek out from behind Davina's four-poster bed, we could tell by the looks on the other kids' faces that they were really jealous of all our brilliant stuff.

We watched anxiously as the school procession arrived at the bottom junction. If they turned right, they wouldn't be able to avoid the main street, and they'd get to the judges before us, but if they turned left they would be heading up the hill towards The Cedars and the outskirts of the village. Slowly, Stanislaw, the leader, released the brake. We watched nervously as his truck trundled forward into the road. Aaaaand – LEFT. He'd turned left! The school were out of the game! TC's plan had worked.

Bert, who seemed to have missed all the drama, folded his paper neatly in a really slow, annoying way and shuffled over to the cab.

"We off, then?" he asked pleasantly.

"We most certainly are," grinned Ryan.

As we neared the main street, I started to get nervous. There was a fairground smell of burger vans and burnt sugar drifting towards us on the breeze, and I could hear a distant murmuring, which I supposed was the crowd. Mine and Boy Dave's Easter bunny costumes were already getting uncomfortable – they were scratchy and the rabbit tummies were padded to make them look fat, so they were really hot as well.

Cautiously I peered round the edge of the truck.

When I'd been daydreaming about being gladiators, I had been a muscled, battle-torn warrior with piercing blue eyes who was used to hordes of cheering people (who, let's face it, weren't real people at all – just adoring masses). What I hadn't been was an Easter bunny about to go very slowly down a completely, completely empty road past the whole population of our village. And the whole population of all the surrounding villages. And several coach-loads of tourists, who you could tell were tourists because they were waving Union Jacks over the sides of the metal barriers, which were holding them all back.

"Well." I tried to sound jolly. "Looks like we're the first."

At the start of the parade route was a group of people in uniform who, for no good reason that I could think of, seemed to be waiting for us. As soon as they saw our truck, they stepped out in front of it and formed three long lines. Seconds later there was the *trrrrrrr rrrrrr rrrr* of a drum roll and the air was filled with spinning batons and jolly whistling marching music. With the band leading us in, we set off at a snail's pace past the crowd.

I said the Women's Institute has to get in on everything, but this was ridiculous. The road was literally lined with hags. For some reason they were all dressed in white bath hats and aprons and carrying baskets full of vegetables. As we passed, they scowled suspiciously and hissed through their teeth with venom tongues.

Luckily (and also not so luckily, as it turned out), it wasn't long before another truck turned into the high street. Across the front was a large blue banner: *Hatton Down Girl Guides 2nd Brigade.*

Ryan peered at it crossly. "This is no good. What are *they* doing here?"

"They must be in the procession as well," I said worriedly.

"Hmm," said Ryan. "Well, I shouldn't think anyone will even look at their rubbish stuff. You can bet your life they haven't got a state-of-the-art egg distributor" (I tried not to catch Boy Dave's eye) "and all this fabulous princess stuff."

But as more and more trucks joined the line, I

started to get a knot in my stomach. What if we didn't win? It was all very well for Ryan to go on about state-of-the-art rabbits, but, being realistic, what with the jolly poo-bear eyes and the purple and pink fur – which, let's face it, didn't entirely cover up his mummifiedness – he was more just a bit of a state. And what if our float was actually a bit too – well – bedroom-ish? What if all the others had really great floats that the judges really liked?

At about the same time as I was thinking this, it started to dawn on me that up until now, me and Boy Dave had never actually appeared in public. We're banned from auditioning for school plays and can't even *go* to school concerts since all the problems with aliens on the science lab roof. We'd been so busy worrying about getting the float ready that we hadn't properly imagined what it would be like, actually being on the back of it, having to win.

And we didn't even dare contemplate what would happen if we didn't.

There was something else I didn't much want to contemplate either. We were starting to go past the first people now, and maybe it was the clicking of cameras, but Boy Dave's padded bottom and perky little white tail suddenly took on a whole new meaning.

"It would be," I swallowed, wishing suddenly that the band were marching us into battle instead, "really good if no one recognized us."

Boy Dave raised his eyes from the deck of the truck, where he had been staring, and flicked them across the crowd.

"I . . ." he said faintly, "really don't think there's much chance of that."

Meanwhile, Ryan, who obviously wasn't having any of the same sorts of doubts, had decided that sitting on his throne wasn't spectacular enough and had begun a sort of royal tour. Flouncing his skirts and throwing flowers from his Easter bonnet, he strutted along the edge of the truck and waved enthusiastically. Liking this, the crowd began to wolf-whistle and cheer encouragingly.

"Come on," said Ryan to us, "they're really enjoying it. Do some rabbity things."

"No, thank you," said Boy Dave. "You're doing quite enough princessy things on your own."

"We'll have to do something, though," I pointed out. "We can't just hide."

"We need something eye-catching," urged Ryan. "Jordan – pretend to ride the pony."

I glanced over to the stable and decided that there are some things you can't do even if your life depends on it. I was about to be really glad I hadn't.

*

Someone yelled out my name, and suddenly three familiar faces were staring up at me. Strangely, though, instead of seeming angry, Mum waved madly and blew kisses, and Dad and Auntie Dulcie goggled and seemed to have gone into shock.

Of course! They didn't know about the cup yet, or any of the other problems. They just thought we were taking part in the Easter Parade. Oh no. My face went red and sweat trickled down my forehead – Dad would never forget.

"Are you sure you wouldn't like a carrot, Jordan?"

"Hop over and fetch me . . . hur, hur, hur" (him laughing).

A lifetime of terrible rabbit jokes stretched ahead of me.

I glanced miserably over to where Ryan had lifted his skirts, jumped on to the throne, jumped off it again and skidded on his knees with his arms out. The air was filled with whistles and laughter and his adoring fans threw back his flowers. Ryan tried to catch them in his teeth at the same time as marching in time to the band.

"Fire them out some Easter eggs," he yelled. "They're loving us."

"Yeah!" yelled Boy Dave back. "In a really *bad way*."

"Come on," I muttered. "It's better than standing around being humiliated."

Pushing up our bunny-ear hoods, we shuffled to the back of the float, where the rabbit was waving and clunking happily. Boy Dave climbed on to the four-poster bed and pulled back the loading drawer.

We fired off quite a few Easter eggs, but it soon became obvious there was a serious design fault with the RPG.

The eggs weren't going into the crowd at all. Instead they were just flying over the top of the cab on to the Girl Guides' truck behind us.

"We'll have to turn it round a bit," I yelled.

Sweating from the bunny costumes, me and Boy Dave heaved and pushed until, with a dodgy sort of inner clunk, the RPG swivelled to the left. This time was better in so much as the eggs went more to the left of the Girl Guides' truck. I felt a bit peeved. They were probably all scoffing them down right this minute and thinking their luck was in.

"More to the left," yelled Boy Dave as we heaved and shoved.

"Is it just me or does the RPG look a bit funny to you?" I asked as we stood back for a breather.

"It's always looked totally weird. Come on, let's give it another go."

"You don't think it's sort of waving a bit . . . well . . . more than it used to?"

"Nah, it's just getting into its stride." Boy Dave climbed up and reloaded. "Come on, let's try it now."

We managed to buzz a few Easter eggs actually into the crowd this time, and it was starting to go quite well. Then I noticed that, for some reason, two extra-large Girl Guides had hefted themselves down off their truck and seemed to be on the way to ours.

A bit late in the day, I remembered what Claire had said about the Girl Guides' rugby team being like the New Zealand All Blacks. It was like two snorting rhinoceroses in uniforms and little blue hats stamping towards us.

"We have no more eggs for you," I told Rhinoceros One as she drew level. "These are for the other people now."

The rhinos pawed the ground, and Rhino One started to climb the ladder.

"Bert!" I banged on the back of the cab. "You have to go faster. There are some seriously huge girls trying to infiltrate our truck."

"You splattered my patrol," snorted Rhino One. "And now I'm going to splatter you."

"Bert!" I hammered frantically on the cab again. "Bert, you must go faster!"

"FLOOR IT," yelled Boy Dave.

We were passing a stall with a big banner saying *Hatton Down Women's Institute Home Produce.* On the other side of the road was a long tent. Up ahead, there was a sudden great twirling and throwing of batons as the majorettes began to march past them. This was terrible. We were seconds away from the judges.

"I'm afraid this is princesses and rabbits only." Boy Dave tried desperately to unpeel Rhino One's fingers from the bar. Meanwhile, Ryan did the worst thing he could have done.

"YOU'RE A CRAZY MAD PERSON WHO IS TOO FAT FOR HER UNIFORM," he yelled at her. "GO AWAY THIS INSTANT."

The effect was spoiled somewhat by our float welcoming her to fairyland.

There was only one thing for it. With a desperate almighty heave me and Boy Dave pushed Rhino One off the steps, on to Rhino Two. They landed in a heap on the ground, and the hags from the Women's Institute stall, who had been watching eagerly like vultures, groaned disappointedly.

"Jordan!" I turned to see Ryan crouched on top of the pony. "Hold my arm. I'm going to somersault off and impress the judges."

We were seconds away from victory. Ryan was on top of the pony. Boy Dave was zooming Easter eggs into the crowd. I was doing a cheerful little rabbit dance . . . when: "Degarriat!" cried a voice. "Smithozilllo!"

And there it was: disaster – literally staring us in the face.

Weirdly enough, Tom didn't seem to have noticed all Davina's bedroom things.

"Where's TC?" he asked as me and Ryan stared at him in horror and Ryan flung his skirt over the horse's head.

"I . . . really have no idea," I told him, trying to block his view with my rabbit tummy.

"I've just been to make sure he delivered the prize cup." Tom looked confused. "He must have got them mixed up and delivered the wrong one."

I looked around frantically, wondering how to get rid of him – which was when I saw it.

"Where's the float with the Carnival King?" I heard Tom ask, as if from a long way away.

"I," I said faintly, "I really have no idea."

As it happened, this wasn't strictly true. Far off in the distance, gliding up Chalky Hill, I had just seen the unmistakable shape of the school's giant brown Easter bunny.

"Oh . . . well. . ." Tom was a bit dazed-seeming

himself. "Heck of a day! I'll catch you later." He clicked his fingers. "Keep it real, team."

It might have been better if he'd said this to TC. For some reason – which, no matter how hard I tried, I couldn't think what it could be – the rest of the Easter Parade was on its way to the golf club.

There wasn't time to worry about it, though. With a sudden surge of nerves, I realized we had stopped, and from behind a table on a long stage, five enquiring faces were gazing right at us.

It was now or never.

We smiled and waved wildly as Boy Dave reloaded madly; then I did my rabbit dance again and Ryan threw himself off the pony.

"I'm all right," he said, trying to stand up, "I'm all right. Help me back on my steed."

That was when the Girl Guides slung him off the truck.

At the exact moment Ryan landed on the table in front of the judges, one of the metal gates that was holding back the crowd came crashing over, and there was a diabolical howl.

"MY FRONE. MY BED. MY SNUGGLIES. MY COOSHUNS. MY HORSEY. MY FUFFYS" (and, a bit unfairly) "MY PWETTY FWOWER HAT."

The judges, who had already been a bit surprised when Ryan landed in front of them, stared over his body at Davina, who was trying to drag him off by his leg.

"Argggh," yelled Bill Leafydew as Ryan grabbed his ponytail and hung on to it as if his life depended on it.

"POOOOOO BUUUM!" yelled Davina.

PC White appeared as if from out of nowhere.

"Right!" He took out his notebook. "That's quite enough of that," he told Davina. "You'll have to get back behind the barrier, and you. . ." He glowered at us. We never got to hear our bit because Davina interrupted him.

"YOU ARE A GREAT BIG STINKY POO!" she informed him as she swung off Ryan's leg and pounded his shins with her feet. "AND A NAPPY FACE, FARTY BUM PLOPPY PANTS. . . THOSE ARE MY FAIRY FIIIIINGS," she yelled at the judges. "AND YOU HAVE WEE COMING OUT OF YOUR EARS AND POO COMING OUT OF YOUR NOSE AND YOUR PANTS ARE FULL OF POO AND YOUR WHOLE HEAD IS A TOILET AND . . . AND. . ."

I lost track of all the other things the judges were because a cauliflower whacked me on the back of the head. I turned round just in time to dodge an aubergine. For some reason, people had started throwing WI vegetables at us.

"It was the Easter eggs," gasped Boy Dave, who

was crouched behind the four-poster bed. "They seem to explode on impac. . ."

He was drowned out by a sudden deafening shattering sound coming from the RPG. At the same time a giant white marrow whistled through the air and the judges' tent collapsed into a writhing heap of canvas. Sticking out of the top of it, Excalibur-style, was the RPG's arm.

"Phew," said Ryan crawling out from underneath. "That was close."

But there was something in the way Boy Dave was staring over my shoulder that made me scared to turn around. When I did there was a crazed, red-faced head with standing-up strands of hair and huge bulging eyes at the top of the ladder to our truck.

*Welcome to a magical fairyland*, said the voice, *where all your—*

But Jefferson interrupted it. "WHAT 'AS YOU DOOOOONE?"

Seconds later we were off the truck and running for our lives.

Those members of the crowd who hadn't received an Easter egg obviously thought this was a lot better than the proper Easter Parade, and they cheered wildly as we bombed back down the main street. Ryan hung on to his Easter bonnet and waved loyally at his fans, but it wasn't really the time for it. Somehow we had to escape from Jefferson and PC White and get up to the golf course to find TC before Tom found him first.

Our break came at the village green, where the crowd thinned back. Boy Dave swerved left and shoved one of the barriers aside.

"Quick, head for the woods."

I think we could all have done with a proper rest, but there was no time to lose. We hacked up through the woods in a semi-circle and came out at the top of the town near the school. By then there was no one following us, so, with me and Boy Dave dripping with sweat from the bunny costumes, we jogged the rest of the way up to Chalky Hill.

When we got there, though, we found ourselves looking up a completely empty road.

"It was probably all the Easter stress you've been under," said Boy Dave sympathetically, "making you hallucinate rabbits everywhere."

"No, I saw them. They were definitely here!"

"They don't seem to be here any more," said Ryan. "Maybe they've already gone."

"But there's nowhere else they can be," I said. "We would have seen them."

We hadn't been in the woods long enough for the whole school procession to pass by without us noticing.

"They must be further up, then," said Boy Dave. "Come on."

Further and further up we climbed, but there was still no sign. Although, as we drew nearer the top, I did think I could hear the faint sound of marching music.

It wasn't until we finally shuffled into the golf club car park that we found TC. He and Brigadier Jones were watching Stanislaw and Whipstaff having an argument. At least it was sort of an argument, except that Whipstaff wasn't actually using words.

"ABALOW WUF ENUMOLUM IMPLEBLOFF!' he bellowed over the sound of what must have been the "to the rear" marching band, who were gathered round a large hole in the fence at the end. The only time I'd ever seen anyone that red in the face was Ryan after his day in the sauna. Stanislaw, on the other hand, looked even more pale than usual and probably had the Christmas feeling from eating TC's idea of a packed lunch.

"Is not possible," he told Whipstaff dismally. "We reverse SEVEN trucks BACK DOWN hill. CANNOT be done. SEVEN trucks," he said again. "BACK DOWN tiny little" – he made a wiggly shape with his finger – "hill!"

"ILLUMMPH, IMMALABLEFORELSEGRASS GREEN!" yelled Whipstaff. "BALLAHMUMSTI-PFUPALLSINABKT!"

During this latest bit of yelling, he jumped round and round in circles before letting out an almighty roar and chasing Stanislaw with his stick.

We went and stood beside TC and Brigadier Jones, who seemed to have made friends.

"Er," I said to TC, "I suppose it's too late to bother mentioning that your dad's looking for you to ask about the other cup."

TC looked over to the golf course, where the carnival procession trucks were all trying to overtake each other really slowly and for no apparent reason.

"They probably won't be needing it now," he said. "The Brigadier thinks it'll be quite a long time before anyone will be able to play golf up here again."

There was a sudden loud bang on the other side of

the car park. Whipstaff stopped trying to behead Stanislaw and shrieked like a man possessed. With arms waving, he rushed towards the lorry as, with a *hiss-clunk*, it trundled forward again through the clubhouse wall.

"Where is the cup, anyway?" asked TC. "Have you won it yet?"

"I'm afraid there were a few problems," explained Ryan. "With a number of exogenous variables."

With another loud crunch the lorry went back over a Mercedes and the convertible roof pinged up into the air like a giant bat's wing. Whipstaff looked as if he was about to burst into tears.

"ROUND ON THE GRASS," yelled Stanislaw to the driver, doing a round-and-round movement with his hand. "YOU NEVER GET OUT OTHERWISE!"

"TC," I asked, "this might sound like a weird question, but *why* did you bring them all up here?"

"Well, I know where this is," explained TC. "I didn't want to get lost. Especially not with Stanislaw; he's really bad-tempered."

"You have a point," said Boy Dave. "But . . . em . . . if you don't mind my saying so, you don't seem to be as worried about everything as maybe . . . you know. Under the circumstances," he added.

"Well, we've been having such a great time," said TC enthusiastically. "It's been like monster trucks. We've been betting 50p's on the damage."

"And," said Brigadier Jones, peering through a pair of field glasses, "talking of which, there goes the putting green. Ten bob to me. They're having to use the golf course to turn round," he explained. "The car park is too narrow. Looks like you're about to make your money back on the goats, though," he told TC. "They're eating the flags. Oh, and here comes Mrs Bagnal and company. They're shooing them away. . . Trying to shoo them away. The one with the horns doesn't want to be shooed. It's turning round . . . off at a gallop. Here comes the other one. Bagnal and company making a run for it – surprisingly good effort . . . goats gaining on them, though. Don't rate their chances. Yes, and . . . good Lord, she won't want to sit down on that for a while." He lowered his glasses. "It's an absolute shambles out there. Rabbit bit the dust a while back. Landed on the princess's head and her crown got wedged over her nose."

"Queen," TC corrected him. "Wedged over the queen's nose."

It was like being behind the scenes at a movie. Dotted across the countryside were little groups of people in flowery hats and costumes, limping dazedly back towards the clubhouse. Joanna, crown still wedged over her face like a weird golden mask, was being guided by Collette and Danielle. Connor, who was running away from the goats, had obviously been made Carnival King at the last moment. He was wearing a gold chain, green tights and puffy velvet trousers.

"Oh wow," said Boy Dave. "This is awesome. We can use it against them for years."

But it was going to take a lot more than Joanna's huge hooter crisis and Connor in velvet to take our minds off the Land Rover that was just turning into the car park.

Before it had even screeched to a halt all the doors flew open and, like something out of *Medal of Honor Airborne*, Jefferson, PC White, Davina and Tom hit the ground, ready for action.

"What are we going to do?" I looked around wildly.

The Land Rover was right in front of the car park exit and so there was no chance of escaping down the hill, but if we tried to hide in the clubhouse we'd be caught like rats (well – rabbits) in a trap.

"When you can't go back, you must go forward," said Brigadier Jones calmly. "Head off across country now and you'll get a head start. Good luck."

On that, me, Boy Dave and Ryan bolted for the hills.

We hared across the golf course in record time and, despite mine and Boy Dave's inconvenient rabbit padding, made it over the stile without a hitch. Ahead of us was the rough, narrow path leading down to the valley, and it was here that I stopped and glanced back. TC and the Brigadier were now sitting on the roof of a golf buggy watching. But apart from that, it all seemed eerily quiet.

For a moment we stared, peering through narrow eyes.

"It doesn't look as if they're. . ." I started to say.

But then we saw them. A line of golf buggies like a convoy of tanks, trundling one by one round the corner of the clubhouse and across the green.

Two dark figures ran ahead of them – Whipstaff and Jefferson, rushing to open the gate. As the buggies passed on to the hills, Whipstaff waved them through with his stick and shouted words of encouragement. On the other side of the gate, Jefferson, his arm in a stiff salute, stood proudly by, whilst back in the car park, with drums rolling and cymbals clashing, the band played them into battle.

It was a bit of a shock to us at first, and looking back on it, pulling down our bunny costumes (and Ryan lifting his skirt), and showing the hunting party our bottoms was probably a bad move.

As we had already found out, golf buggies are surprisingly fast and could probably keep going a lot longer than humans. And TC had already proved they were pretty tough.

"If we can get over that next fence," panted Boy Dave as we reached the flat grass of the valley, "they'll have to stop. There's no one to let them through."

But it was easier said than done. The buggies were really fast on the flat and the gap between them and us was getting smaller all the time.

"TALLY HO!" cried the hunting party as they charged in for the kill.

"Hurry UP," I yelled.

We only just made it. By the time we had scrambled over the stile, my legs were shaking like jelly and the fence had gone a funny shade of blue and was wobbling like a pinged washing line. It must have been all the running making me weird, because by then, I was thinking it was a time portal.

Boy Dave had been right, though. Seconds later the buggies ground to a halt, and a really peeved-looking Mrs Bagnal was glaring daggers at us over the fence.

We took it easier up the rest of the hill, and I had just about realized that I wasn't from the future when Boy Dave's phone rang. Maybe it was because it was one of those days where nothing seemed to happen for the best, but as he fished for it inside his rabbit sleeve and said, "Wonder who that is", I realized that I really didn't want to know.

Boy Dave clicked his phone shut and stared frowning at the horizon.

"That was weird," he said at last.

Listening to his side of the conversation had been weird too. Boy Dave had said "Hello, hello" a couple of times and then just listened with a puzzled look on his face.

"And?" I asked. "Who?"

"Well. . . It sounded like TC and Tom. There was someone else there but I don't know who that was. They all sounded really far off."

"Far off is good," I said with feeling. "Maybe TC hit speed dial without knowing it. I did that once and Mum heard a whole lot of iffy stuff."

"Bit of a coincidence, though," said Ryan. "I mean – that it was Boy Dave's number."

"That's the weird thing," said Boy Dave. "TC was telling Tom about the games, but obviously Tom wasn't interested. And then someone else said 'Turn left here', so I think they were in a car."

None of this sounded particularly interesting. Me and Boy Dave must have sweated pints trying to run in the rabbit costumes and I was really hot and thirsty. Right then all I wanted to think about was ice-cold swimming pools and fizzy drinks.

We had reached the top of the hill, and down below the sun bounced off the dirt track like a chalk scribble on the fields. In front of us birds wheeled and dipped in the wind. As the wind blew past my ears it made a peaceful sort of *shkk, shkk, shkk* sound.

"Well, it doesn't matter now," I told Boy Dave.

But he still wouldn't let it go.

"It's just that TC said something really weird."

"How surprising!"

"That's what I'm trying to tell you," said Boy Dave crossly. "It was about the only weird thing he *couldn't* have said."

A tiny black dot had appeared on the chalk track below. Boy Dave's pretty good with cars – he can tell what they are just by the headlights – and it must have taken his mind off TC because he said suddenly, "That's a Land Rover."

We watched for a moment as the little black dot drew nearer. Drivers always do go slowly along there because the road is lumpy, with holes and ditches. But this car was going really slowly even for that. As if the driver was looking for something. Or someone. Me and Ryan were slow to suss it out but Boy Dave suddenly banged his hand on his head.

"Oh NO! That's what TC was on about. He told Tom that the Undertaker was the best character to be in *Car Chase*." By now we had reluctantly broken into a run. "And I heard that bit really clearly," he yelled over his shoulder, "because he shouted it."

"Well," puffed Ryan as we caught up, "there's no way TC would have made a mistake like that."

It was true. The one thing TC would never get confused about was which characters belonged in which games. They were practically tattooed on his brain. The Undertaker, *Car Chase* – he couldn't have picked a better way of putting it.

They were heading us off.

A clump of bushes lay about half a mile ahead. But we knew deep down it was hopeless. The Land Rover was only a bend away and we stood out on the hillside like targets. We'd never beat a car, no matter how slowly it was going. And by now we'd guessed who the other person was. Maybe if we hadn't just run the best part of three miles, we could have outrun

PC White up the hill again, but not now. There was nowhere to go and nowhere to hide. The game was well and truly over.

Just to rub it in, a tractor, which must have been coming in the other direction down the track, turned on to the field. As we ran towards it, the driver yelled, "Hoi, there's no footpath here."

A man with purple cheeks who looked a lot like a turnip scarecrow poked his head out the side. He gave me a hard look.

"It's Dom Smith's lad, isn't it?"

"Erm. . ." I said nervously, trying to remember if I'd had any problems with a man who looked like a turnip lately. "Probably not."

The turnip man beckoned me over, and his attitude had completely changed.

"Ray Chiggley." He held out his hand. "If, perchance, you do turn out to be him, I owe you a debt of gratitude."

It was the tiniest slimmest chance, but the way I saw it, we'd been having bad fate as far back as I could remember. If this was good fate at long last, then bring it on.

"Actually, there is something," I told him. "We'd like a ride in your tractor. Right now."

Ray Chiggley's eyes almost fell out of his purple head as we piled into his old one-man Fergie, but I suppose he found it a bit difficult to tell us he'd changed his mind.

"Been to the carnival, then?" he asked cautiously. And when no one answered, "I'm going into the village to pick up some silage, if that's any good to you?"

We went the long route, up the same hill we had just run over and across the top fields above the valley. I managed to get on to the step and hang on the side like a real farmhand.

The proud feeling didn't last, though. As we neared the village I had a sudden flashback to the farmer's jeep appearing over the brow of the hill that day when TC trawled his sheep. We were about to appear in exactly the same way.

"Perhaps," I suggested, "it would be best if you just dropped us here."

"Can't drop you *here*," said Ray Chiggley cheerfully. "No footpath. Farmer would shoot you.

And then he'd shoot me." (For some reason he seemed to find this funny.) He had obviously mistaken our fear for us trying to be considerate because he added, "It's no bother."

"Thank you," we whispered as we cowered in the bottom of the tractor.

It was the strangest thing, though. We'd expected the golf club to be the same as when we left it, but I suppose quite a lot of time had gone by since then. Although bits of rubble lay strewn about and there were a few cars, including Whipstaff's Merc with its bat wing, there was absolutely no sign of any people at all.

"Be-limey," said Ray Chiggley as we bumped down the road past the car park. "Looks like someone's been up here with a bulldozer."

"Yes," we said feebly. "Gosh."

Maybe it was the sight of the big gaping hole in the clubhouse wall, but I suddenly had what felt like the best idea ever.

"Do you think I could get off for a minute? Only my sister was up here earlier and I'd just like to make sure . . ." (I tried to force the words out) ". . . make sure she's all right." Boy Dave and Ryan spluttered. "I mean, that she isn't still here," I said hurriedly.

As soon as the tractor stopped I jumped down and ran to the hole in the wall. Boy Dave and Ryan looked after me in amazement as I disappeared through it, but I couldn't say what was really on my mind. The clubhouse bar! Boy, would the others be pleased to see me when I got back with a rabbit costume full of fizzy drink and snacks!

The hole in the wall led into a corridor. Even though the place seemed completely empty, I tiptoed quietly just in case. I had made it within spitting distance of the bar when I heard a faint click up ahead. As if someone was softly closing a door.

I should have got out then and there, but it seemed so weird. And by then I was beginning to understand what had made Ryan think it was OK to casually walk past TC's mum while she was on the toilet. I'd been daydreaming of lemonade ever since the hill (which is weird because I normally like orange) and I wasn't prepared to give up that easily.

Just before the bar was a room with the door open and I supposed the click had come from there. As quietly as I could, I crept towards it and peeked through the gap where the hinges joined. It was with a small sigh of relief that I recognized the tall, straight back of Brigadier Jones. He was standing at a table putting large wedges of money into a bin liner.

When you see something out of the ordinary, you think some really silly things. My first thought was to wonder why was he throwing all that money away. Then I wondered why he was putting it all in a bin liner if he wasn't going to throw it away. I was just wondering whether to say hello or to try and sneak past him when, without turning round, he said, "Come in."

He said this in a really normal-sounding voice, as if putting money in bin liners was something that he did every day.

"Good," he said calmly as I poked my head nervously round the door. "You made it. Where are the others?"

He wandered over to the door and looked up and down the corridor.

"They're. . ." I stopped myself. There's a kind of rule that you say you're on your own. This is normally for when you might be in trouble, but I suppose it was just habit. "Gone home," I finished.

"Well, I'm finished tidying up here," said the Brigadier. "I'd rather not have money lying around in an unsecured building; you never know who might try and get their hands on it."

"I know it's a bit of a cheek," I said timidly, "but before you go, would you mind if I just went down to the bar and got something to drink and a packet of crisps?"

"I'll get them for you." The Brigadier hoisted the bin liners off the table. "It's not safe for you to be wandering around. You wait here." And with that he took the bin liners, left the room and locked the door behind him.

At first I thought it was just an accident: like he'd locked the door automatically without thinking, but after a few minutes I started to panic.

"Hey!" I yelled, rattling the handle loudly in the silence. "Unlock the door."

It wasn't as if I'd be in there for long, I told myself; the others would soon wonder where I'd got to and. . . The others. I stopped. The Brigadier had thought I was on my own when he locked me in. For all he knew I'd have been there all night. I felt the hair prickle on the back of my neck. Either he was going to call PC White – not very likely, seeing as he'd helped us escape in the first place – or he'd been lying about the money. Either way, I wasn't going to hang round and wait to be rescued. For all I knew, once he spotted Boy Dave and Ryan, they could be in danger.

Up until then it had been a bit like a film, but this next bit wasn't. There was a small window at the back of the office with thick, frosted glass. In films when there's a fire or something they always panic and throw a chair through a window at the last minute (and no, I didn't do it straightaway either). If you want to break a window in real life it's much easier. I ripped off my rabbit costume and wrapped it as thickly as I could around my arm and hand. Then I thumped hard on the glass a couple of times.

It shattered on the second blow. Hurriedly I punched out the jagged bits, unwrapped the rabbit costume and laid it over the sill before climbing out.

The first thing the others knew about any of it was when I charged towards them, naked except for my pants, shouting, "The Brigadier, the Brigadier!" at the top of my voice.

Before I had time to explain, and before they had time to ask all the questions they so obviously wanted to ask, a car screeched round from behind the clubhouse and swerved wide towards the cliff edge. With a screeching wheel spin it recovered in the nick of time and curved towards the top of Chalky Hill.

"Stop him!" I yelled. "Stop him."

When Ray Chiggley said he owed me a debt of gratitude, he couldn't have known it would turn out like this, but he must have had some faith in me after what happened because he released the brake and the tractor rolled forward to block the road.

Too late.

It's true that life goes into slow motion. I saw the

Brigadier's car. I worked out where the tractor was. I looked at the Brigadier's car again – and all this seemed very easy, as if I had plenty of time. I heard the long drawn-out squeal of brakes and then the bang. It was endless, like glass and metal crunching away into infinity.

When I took my hands away from my eyes, the front of the Brigadier's car was concertinaed against the side of the Fergie and Ray Chiggley was staring as if his eyes were going to pop out of his head. Boy Dave and Ryan had already thrown themselves out the other side. As they staggered round to greet me, the door on the driver's side of the car swung open.

"Look out!" I yelled.

The Brigadier half fell and half crawled out of his car.

"My goodness," he said in a voice that was really weird for someone who's crawling on all fours, "that was one hell of a prang."

"He's got the money," I told Ray Chiggley. "And he locked me in a room."

Ray Chiggley stared from one to the other of us as the Brigadier, propping himself up on the roof, made his way round to the boot of the car.

"Well, one can't leave money around in an unsecured building," he said as casually as when he'd said it to me. "I'm sorry about that damned door; it's always been a problem."

Boy Dave and Ryan stared at me and my mouth fell open. There was no way Ray Chiggley would believe me over him. Even I was starting to think I'd imagined things.

Then I saw a sight I never thought I'd be glad to see. On the other side of the tractor a car was coming up the road. Seconds later Tom's Land Rover crawled to a halt and PC White stepped out, followed by Tom. I didn't think it would help much but I said to PC White, "He's got all the money in bin liners."

To my surprise, PC White nodded. "The safe is alarmed straight to the police station. My secretary called almost as soon as it was opened."

Even then the Brigadier might have been able to talk his way out of it, but we found out later that it wasn't just the golf course. He was wanted for conning loads of groups out of money. If he'd hung around, as PC White was going to make him do, it would only be a matter of time before they found out who he really was. So he did the only thing he could do. He tried to make a run for it.

For all his cheerfulness, Ray Chiggley didn't hang about. As soon as he realized what was happening, he jumped down from his cab and hared after the Brigadier. Seconds later his fist shot out and the next thing we knew, the Brigadier was on the ground trying to make snow angels without the snow.

I couldn't say we were exactly heroes after that,

although it was nice for Ray Chiggley because, although his son was a petty thief, he had stopped a worse one. As for us, we were "a bunch of stupid idiots and anything might have happened and la la", but this was a lot better than what they would have been saying if all the stuff with the Brigadier had never happened. He was the treasurer for the golf club and if all the problems with the Easter Parade hadn't happened, and he hadn't taken his chance when he did, he would probably just have disappeared one day with the money and never been caught.

When everyone else had left earlier to have cups of tea and things, he'd stayed on and cleared out all the golf club bank accounts on the computer. Then he'd bagged all the on-site cash and trophies. He hadn't realized Whipstaff had set the alarm on the safe before he went.

It's funny how things change. The Brigadier had turned out to be nothing like he seemed at first, and TC. . . Well. . .

As soon as his face appeared like a nervous white blob round the side of the tractor we all yelled "TC!" at the tops of our voices and were really glad to see him.

Tom lent me his not-very-nice pink jumper, and while PC White put handcuffs on the Brigadier and checked the boot of his car, we wandered over to the edge of the hill and sat looking out over Hatton Down.

"I knew you would know," TC told Boy Dave. "I couldn't say much at the time because Dad and PC White made me go with them. They dropped Davina off, but they wanted to keep an eye on me." He sounded really proud about this.

"It was lucky you managed to speed dial me and not someone else," said Boy Dave. "That must have been tricky."

There was a moment's unexpected silence; then TC blinked and cleared his throat.

"Not really. There's only one number in my phone." He stuck his chin out bravely. "You're the first real friend I've ever had."

The sun was getting lower in the sky now and the rooftops of the village looked orange and warm in the spring dusk.

"Friends," I corrected him. "And we're really glad we are."

There is mostly a happy ending to this story, with one sad bit. (Although even that didn't turn out to be too sad in the end.) The sad bit is that TC's family moved quite soon afterwards. This wasn't just because of what happened. Apparently, after the exorcist had gone, his mum kept having nasty experiences with three shadowy black figures in hats who waved a broom at her, and Isabelle mysteriously disappeared. (Although all her things disappeared at the same time, so the only person who thought she'd met a sticky end was TC's mum, and even she didn't seem too upset about it.)

Talking of people disappearing, Brigadier Jones pretended to be a prison inspector, was given tea by the prison governor, and then was never seen again. We never found out if he was a real brigadier. I expect he's something else these days.

Now I'm going to be grown-up about this next bit and just tell it really seriously. Joanna had to have her crown sawed off at the hospital. Apparently the doctor said it was like a sort of arrow effect, whereby the crown went over Joanna's nose quite easily, but then got caught on the sticking-out bit of her *huge hooter* (I'm only saying what he said) and wouldn't come off again. Still, like I told her, she might not have got the chance to be Carnival Queen, but at least she still got her picture in the paper. Joanna was in the middle (as usual), with Collette and Danielle smiling and pretending to try and pull the crown off. The headline was really exciting (not). It said: *Carnival Queen Gets Crown Stuck.* They could have had *Enormous Conk in Carnival Crisis*, but there you go.

As for our dads, they found it all a bit confusing. It was like they thought they should be blaming us for something but they weren't really sure what. At the same time they thought they should be quite proud of us as well. And also angry (but what's new). I think Tom bought Davina a life-sized wooden playhouse for the garden to make up for her room.

Obviously the school were very disappointed, as they kept saying over and over again, especially as it meant no one was willing to come and judge the hanging-baskets competition in the summer. Still, Tom donated some computers to the school before TC left, and getting something for free always makes the headmistress happy.

Tom ended up happy too. After they moved, TC

persuaded him to start a business with a real-live computer-type game in an old warehouse. TC thinks up all the games and they have cool lasers, electronic moving floors, a massive sound system and loads of other good gadgets. Tom has started a campaign called "Keep it Real" and parents bring their kids from all over the country to teach them real-live actions and experiences again. He was on TV the other day talking about it. TC emailed to invite us all up to have a go of the warehouse and mentioned that Tom even has a publicity agent now called Jasper.

So it came to be that TC had a leaving party. And this time it was me, Boy Dave and Ryan who organized it for him in the woods. We had a bit of help from our own dads. Unfortunately they tried to give me and Boy Dave bits of lettuce and kept saying things like, "D'you want it well done or hare?", "Bunny thing happened the other day", "Bob's your uncle", as well as the usual hop-and-jump stuff.

Honestly, I think they must have sat in the café one morning and worked them all out specially. Still, at least they did the decent thing and hid behind the barbecue for the whole time and avoided talking to anyone who wasn't their own age.

Oh, and Claire took me fishing.

Read all about Jordan, Boy Dave
and Ryan's earlier adventures!

MAD, BAD & UTTERLY BARMY!